YOU COME TO YOKUM

Carol Otis Hurst

with illustrations by Kay Life

Houghton Mifflin Company Boston 2005

Walter Lorraine Books

For Betty and the tellers of the tales of Yokum

Walter Lorraine *wn* Book

Text copyright © 2005 by Carol Otis Hurst
Illustrations copyright © 2005 by Kay Life

www.houghtonmifflinbooks.com

Library of Congress Cataloging-in-Publication Data

Hurst, Carol Otis.
  You come to Yokum / Carol Otis Hurst ; [illustrations by] Kay Life.
    p. cm.
  "Walter Lorraine books."
  Summary: Twelve-year-old Frank witnesses his mother's struggles to
muster support for women's right to vote even as the family's life is
transformed by a year running a lodge in western Massachusetts in the
early 1920s.
  ISBN-13: 978-0-618-55122-4 (hardcover)
  ISBN-10: 0-618-55122-0 (hardcover)
  1. Women—Suffrage—United States—Juvenile fiction. [1. Women—
Suffrage—Fiction. 2. Feminists—Fiction. 3. Family life—
Massachusetts—Fiction. 4. Hotels, motels, etc.—Fiction. 5.
Massachusetts—History—20th century—Fiction.] I. Life, Kay, ill. II.
Title.
  PZ7.H95678Yo 2005
  [Fic]—dc22
                                                            2005001228

Printed in the United States of America
QUM 10 9 8 7 6 5 4 3 2 1

CONTENTS

YOU COME TO YOKUM

MOTHER

Hurry, hide the women
Cuz Grace is at the door
She talks and talks and talks
And then she talks some more.
Hide your daughters and your aunties
And you'd better hide your goat
Cuz Grace is at the door again
She wants them all to vote.

That's our mother they were talking about in that rhyme. I don't know who made it up, but Jim and I must have heard it a thousand times. We got upset the first few times, and there were a few scuffles over it, but after a while we just ignored it. That chant was just part of the kidding we took about our mother and, although he never came right out and said so, Dad must have taken his share of lumps from the other farmers in the small town of Montgomery, Massachusetts, where we lived.

She did sometimes go door to door handing out political pamphlets. That made her very different from the other women we knew.

Back then most women didn't say much in public about politics. They had other things to think about. Their job was to care for children and husbands, to put out three square meals a day, keep a clean house, and leave the politicking to the men. Other women must have had opinions about what they read in the papers, but mostly they let the men do the talking when it came to politics.

My mother, you understand, did all those things I mentioned: she kept house; she was a pretty good cook—nothing to compare with Aunt Winnie, of course, but we always managed to put away most of what she put before us. She tended the house and us, and Dad took care of the farm.

It wasn't much of a farm—just a few dairy cattle. The land in Montgomery wasn't much good for raising crops. Dad always said the only crop you could be sure of raising when you plowed a field in Montgomery was rocks. Stone walls outlining every field around were testimony to that. So we had a garden every year and raised enough vegetables, which Mother put up, to carry us through the winter what with the chickens, a pig, and a steer for meat.

Mother was a suffragist. She wanted women to have the right to vote, and she said so loudly and clearly every chance she got. She handed out pamphlets everywhere, much to our embarrassment. She went off to meetings and came home full of enthusiasm for the next one. We knew that some women in England and in the United States went much further than that —chaining themselves to fences and marching through the streets. The newspapers made a lot of it. Jim and I didn't pay it much attention. I don't know that Dad did either, really. He fretted some and muttered a bit, but that was just Dad.

Sometimes his muttering threw our friends a bit. They'd see him walking around in circles in the drive or the kitchen muttering, and they'd try to make sense of what he was saying. One time Chet Warner came by when I was still doing chores. When I came into the kitchen, Dad was muttering, and Chet was very excited.

"Wait!" he protested as I tried to lead him away. "Your father said something about the Democrats burning down Washington. And I couldn't make out what he said the Russians have done."

So Jim and I took some kidding about Dad's muttering and Mother's politicking, but everybody got teased about something or someone. It was just part of being a kid—like getting Indian burns when they twisted the skin on your forearm in different directions, sore fannies when you went through the hotbox, and sore muscles in your arm when they gave you noogies for not saying "noog out!" fast enough. We gave as good as we got, you understand—teasing and torturing with the best of them.

Jim and I thought, if we thought about it at all, that Mother's politicking was just part of Mother. Being teased about it was just one of those things you get used to. It really didn't matter very much.

But everything changed in the winter of 1920. And it all started with the Model T.

THAT TARNATIOUS MACHINE

"Where's Dad, Frank?"

"In the barn, currying Prince."

"Wish he'd hurry up," Jim said. "Uncle Clint will be here any minute."

"Not until eleven." I tried to sound calm, but I knew Jim heard the squeak in my voice.

We'd had a spell of warm weather lately—the January thaw, I guess. It had been well above freezing for the last five days, and today the thermometer on the barn read 55 degrees; of course, that was in the sun. Still, it was nice not to have to bundle up as much as usual.

Jim wasn't even trying to hide his excitement. He'd been dancing around the dooryard for the past hour, stopping only to run into the house every few minutes to look at the grandfather clock in the front hall. I suppose I was as bad as that when I was ten. Now that I was practically a teenager, I just paced back and forth the way Dad did when there was something on his mind—without the muttering, of course.

We turned to see my father walking up the driveway from the barn, stepping carefully to avoid both the ice and the puddles where things had melted.

Jim ran to him. "It's almost time, Dad. Aren't you excited?"

"Excited?" My father spoke the word as if he'd never heard it before. He shook his head. "Pshaw! No, I'm not excited."

He looked down at Jim without breaking stride as he headed toward the house.

"Nothing to be excited about, Jim. It's a machine, for goodness' sake. You just start it up and steer the foolish thing. Takes no skill. Nothing like what it takes to handle a horse. I don't know why you all are making so much of this."

We were making so much of it because no one had expected this day would ever come. My father was a horseman—the best in Montgomery, people said. One touch of his hand or even the murmur of his voice would calm a nervous mare or a skittish colt. People for miles around called on my father to break a new horse or to settle a difficult one. No one knew quite how he did it. He'd talk to the horse softly and pet it a bit, and the next thing you knew, that horse would take the bit without a fuss and that would be it.

We were proud of our own horses. Our wagons and carriages were in better shape than most people's houses. The sight of my father heading out with Prince, our black Morgan, hitched up to the buggy or sleigh—harness gleaming, every bit of brass glinting in the sun, Prince stepping high, clean and brushed, hooves polished—well, that was something. Even our big workhorses, Patch and Samson, were always brushed and combed before Dad hitched them up to the plow or harrow.

My father behind the wheel of a motorcar, however, was something else again. Lots of folks in Montgomery and all around western Massachusetts had automobiles by that time, but Dad refused to have anything to do with what he called "those tarnatious machines." He gave autos a wide berth and a look of contempt when they passed him on the road. He refused to acknowledge the drivers even when they were his good friends.

My father complained to anyone who would listen that motorcars were an invention of the devil. They scared the horses with their noise and dirt. He vowed never to go near one.

When Dad's brother Clint bought a Model T Ford as a Christmas present for himself and Aunt Winnie and offered to teach my father to drive it, Dad's response was a loud snort.

He was leaving the room in disgust but stopped short when my mother said, "I'll do it if you won't, Fred."

There was dead silence as we all turned disbelieving eyes on Mother.

She nodded as if agreeing with herself. "If we had an auto, Fred, we could get to Westfield in no time instead of spending half the day with the horse." She took on that determined look we'd all learned to dread. "Fred," she said. "I mean it. I'll do it if you won't."

"You'll do what?" asked my father.

"Learn to drive," said my mother. She was looking straight at him.

Mother seldom spoke up to my father in front of us kids except about women's suffrage, of course, although we'd heard her light into him when she thought we were asleep or off somewhere.

"A woman, drive a motorcar? Nonsense!"

"It's not nonsense!" she said. "There's nothing about driving a motorcar a woman can't do, is there, Clint?"

I looked from my father to Uncle Clint. At first glance, there was a similarity. Both were tall and thin with reddish hair and moustaches. The main difference was in their usual expressions. Uncle Clint often had a grin on his face while Dad was of a more serious nature.

But Uncle Clint wasn't grinning then. His head was swiveling back and forth between my mother and his brother. He knew better than to speak, and he didn't have to.

"No wife of mine is going to drive a motorcar! If anyone in this family is to drive a tarnatious machine, it'll be me," my father said, cutting off further discussion.

So, this very morning, Uncle Clint was going to teach my father how to drive.

Word had spread. As the time approached, neighbors

gathered in our dooryard enjoying any excuse to socialize and be outside for a change. Rex greeted them all, tail wagging. He wasn't much of a watchdog, but he surely did love company. He went from family to family, getting his pats and praise wherever he could.

My mother stepped out of the back door. Her long coat was unbuttoned, and you could see that she still had her apron on underneath. She looked surprised to see everyone, and she quickly buttoned up her coat before she joined in the general chatter as still more people came up the drive.

"Is he really going to do it?" Chet Warner asked. "Is your father really going to learn to drive an auto?"

"Course he is," said Jim. "My father can do anything."

We all turned as the automobile came round the bend in the road.

"Here he is! Dad, he's here!" Jim ran into the house, slamming the door behind him. He was back out in a minute, one foot on the porch and the other on the step, trying to be in both places at once, and anxious not to miss anything. The automobile won out, and Jim joined the rest of us in the driveway.

Uncle Clint pulled in just off the road and sounded the horn: *Ah-ooh-gah*. Aunt Winnie was sitting beside him.

"Bring it on up," I hollered over the engine noise as I ran toward them. Rex ran beside me, barking loudly and wagging his tail.

Uncle Clint hollered back. "Best to leave it where he's got

plenty of straightaway till he gets the hang of it." He turned off the motor and stepped onto the running board and then down into the driveway. For a minute he looked puzzled at the sight of all the neighbors, but then he grinned and waved.

"We'll start him off slow. Forward first. Then I'll teach him to back up." He turned to wipe his fingerprints off the side of the Ford with a rag. "Better get out, Winnie. Fred will be anxious enough."

Aunt Winnie always did make my father nervous, and some people couldn't see why. She seldom argued with him or with anybody else, for that matter, but she did have a tendency to burst into tears.

"Grace!" Dad would call if Mother was out of the room at such times. "Come see to Winnie."

Even when the conversation was on cheerful matters, my father kept a cautious eye on Winnie, as if she might burst into tears at any minute, and since she cried when she was happy as well as when she was upset, she often did.

Aunt Winnie had been born and brought up in Chicopee, where her father was a shoemaker. I guess they'd stayed pretty much to themselves in the city, at least Aunt Winnie had. She was shy around strangers.

Life on a farm couldn't have been easy for a city girl like Aunt Winnie. She was afraid of any animal except a cat and some dogs. Even the chickens scared her. She claimed there was one rooster that had it in for her. When that rooster became Sunday dinner, she swore another one took up the cause. So Uncle Clint kept all the critters out of her way as much as he could. Uncle Clint even collected the eggs. We'd have kidded him more about that, but no one wanted to hurt Aunt Winnie's feelings. They didn't have any children so both she and Uncle Clint made a lot of Jim and me.

Aunt Winnie was all bundled up, but she loosened the scarf around her neck as Uncle Clint opened her door. She gave him her hand as she stepped down from the automobile. Then she and my mother hugged.

"Never thought I'd see this day," Aunt Winnie said, shaking her head. "How'd you do it, Grace?"

"Why, it was Fred's decision. I had nothing to do with it," Mother said.

Aunt Winnie gave her a look that showed she didn't believe that for a minute.

The neighbors all clustered around the splendid machine, gazing in wonder as Uncle Clint pointed out its features—the gleaming black body matched by the spokes on the wheels, the black leather seats, the brass trim on the gas headlights.

"Not bad for five hundred and twenty-five dollars," Bud Warner said.

"Now, you be patient, Clint," said my mother. "We don't want to discourage Fred."

"He'll do fine, Grace. There's really nothing to it." Uncle Clint looked around. "Where is he?"

"He'll be here in a minute. He's getting changed," Jim said.

"Changed?" Uncle Clint exclaimed. "What's he changing for?"

"He said he intends to go to town once he gets it going."

Uncle Clint shook his head. "We're not going that far. We'll just go up and down the drive a few times. Then we'll go down the road a piece, but we won't stop to call on anybody."

The back door opened and my father stepped out.

"Now step to the side, ladies and gentlemen. Clear the way! New driver approaching!" Uncle Clint grinned widely as he made a sweeping bow, and the crowd stepped back.

Dad shot him a scornful glance. His moustache was combed and waxed. He had on his good Chesterfield overcoat over his navy blue pinstriped suit. His high black shoes shone. The brushed, black derby hat sat squarely on his head.

Ignoring his audience, Dad's eyes fastened directly on the Model T. He fended off Rex's attempt to jump up on him, without taking his eyes off the Ford.

"Get down, you foolish thing!" my father said as he brushed any paw prints from his overcoat. He slid a bit on the icy spot on the drive but quickly regained his footing. Rex headed back to Jim for reassuring pats.

"All right, Fred," Uncle Clint said. "You sit right here behind the wheel, and we'll have you chugging down the road in no time."

My father climbed in and carefully adjusted his coat as he

sat. He grabbed the wheel tightly with both hands.

Uncle Clint stepped up onto the running board.

"Look down at your feet, Fred," Uncle Clint directed, pointing at the floor.

Those of us in front leaned forward.

"This pedal on the left is the brake. This one in the middle is reverse. We won't use that one right away so ignore it for now."

"Ignore the one in the middle," Jim said.

Uncle Clint went on. "This one on the right makes the car go forward. That's the one you're going to push ever so gently once we've got it started. Got it?"

"Ever so gently," Jim said.

Dad twisted his head to locate the various pedals and nodded.

"What's this thing on the running board?" Jim asked, pointing to a brass tank.

"That's the generator for the lights, Jim. We won't be needing them this morning. Now don't distract the driver," Uncle Clint added as my father craned his neck, trying to see the generator.

Dad frowned at Jim before quickly turning back to the steering wheel. "Don't ask foolish questions," he said.

"Yeah, don't ask foolish questions," I said. Jim gave me a poke with his elbow. I gave him a shove back and then caught Mother's warning glance. We turned our attention back to the driving lesson.

Uncle Clint reached into the back seat and took out a hard rubber handle.

"What's that?" Dad asked nervously, his hands still tight on the steering wheel.

"It's the crank, Fred. I'll use it in a minute when we're ready to start up." Uncle Clint's voice was soft, as if speaking to a young child. "Now that's the hand brake there by your left hand, Fred. When I tell you to, you'll release it just by pulling up on it a little bit, see, and then lowering it. Now turn on the key."

"Stand back!" my father hollered as he turned the key. There was a whirring sound.

"Good!" said Uncle Clint. "Now set the spark."

"The spark! What spark?" Dad yelled although there was no need to.

"That lever right here on the wheel sets the spark, Fred. Set it about halfway." Uncle Clint's voice was calm as he pointed to a lever on the steering wheel.

"You've got to have the spark right," Jim informed the rest of us.

"Stand back!" yelled my father as he pulled up on the spark lever. There was a slight click.

"You've got it," Uncle Clint said encouragingly.

"He's got it," Jim said.

"Now pull this lever down; that's the throttle. You need to give it the gas. Great! That's enough," Uncle Clint said.

"He's got enough gas," Jim assured us all.

"Now, when I tell you to," Uncle Clint said, "you're going to press very gently on that pedal on the right and hold the wheel straight, and we'll go ahead till we get up to the barn. Then I'll show you how to back up." Uncle Clint stepped off the running board and approached the front of the car. He placed the crank on the shaft in between the headlights. "All set, Fred?"

"Stand back!" Dad yelled again. We dutifully took a step back. Dad was grasping the wheel as if it were a bull fighting to get loose. "Ready," he said between clenched teeth.

"Now don't do anything until I tell you to, Fred." Uncle Clint turned to address the crowd. "Keep your fingers crossed that it doesn't backfire."

We held up crossed fingers as Uncle Clint gave it a quick crank. Nothing happened. He tried again, and this time the motor caught. There was a puff of smoke from the rear of the car.

"Now gently release the hand brake," Uncle Clint said.

"The what?"

"The hand brake!" we all called out. "Release the hand brake."

Dad looked confused. His hands were still on the steering wheel.

"It's right there on your left, Fred. Remember?" Uncle Clint said. He walked around the car to the driver's side. "Just take your left hand off the wheel for a minute. It'll be all right. You're going to pull up on the brake just a trifle and then lower it." He stepped up onto the running board again. "That's it. Now gently, gently now, step on the accelerator."

The car lurched forward as Dad jammed his foot down on the pedal. The jolt knocked Uncle Clint off the running board. He recovered quickly and ran alongside as the Model T picked up speed.

"Stop!" Uncle Clint hollered. "Fred! Hit the brake, Fred! The brake! Pull up on the brake!"

People began to shout, "Hit the brake, Fred!" Rex ran alongside the Ford, barking loudly.

Above the roar of the motor, the barking of Rex, and the shouts of the crowd, we heard my father yelling, "Whoa! Whoa!" as he pulled back against the wheel with all his might.

The Model T approached the barn at forty miles an hour.

"Oh, my land!" said my mother, her hands on her cheeks.

For a moment it seemed that only Uncle Clint was capable of speech. He ran after the car, waving his arms, yelling, and slipping now and again on the wet ice, "Ease up! Ease up, Fred. Hit the brake!"

The answer floated back to the audience in the dooryard: "Whoooooooa!"

My father's back arched, and he pulled back so far it seemed that the steering wheel must come off in his hand. The car zoomed through the open barn doors. There Rex stopped and

sat down. Uncle Clint came to stand beside the dog as the car continued through the barn at full speed.

There was a moment of silence and then a loud crash as the back of the barn gave way.

"Fred!" yelled my mother. "Dear Lord! We've killed him."

Strange sounds came from behind Aunt Winnie's hands, which were clasped over her face.

Only the back wheels of the auto could be seen sticking out of the broken boards at the rear wall of the barn.

Jim and I ran back around the outside of the barn in time to see my father step out of the still-chugging Model T, the front wheels buried in a snow bank. He dusted his hat against his pant leg.

"Tarnatious machine!" he said, and started toward the house. He opened the door and then paused. "See to Winnie, Grace," he said.

Uncle Clint looked at my mother. "I think we'll leave your lesson until tomorrow, Grace. My nerves are shot."

JAIL TIME

"Think Mother will be all right driving all the way to Washington?" Jim asked. When Jim bent down to add his snowball to the pile, you could see his raw, chapped wrists in the space where the mittens ended and his sleeves began. Mine were just the same. Mother had offered to make longer wrists on our mittens to prevent this painful condition, but no self-respecting kid would wear that kind of mitten. That would be as bad as letting her stitch them onto our sleeves as she often said she would if we kept losing them. We put up with the chapped and bleeding wrists every winter just like all the rest of the kids.

"You heard Uncle Clint. He said Mother learned quickly and was as good as he was after only three lessons." I was proud of my mother's driving skill, although careful not to say so around my father. "Besides, she's only driving to Springfield," I told Jim. "She'll catch the train from there to Washington."

"What if it snows?"

"Dad says no snow till tomorrow. She'll be in Washington by then." My father studied the clouds and the weathervane on the barn roof every morning and was seldom wrong about the weather forecast.

The cold had returned with a vengeance after the January thaw and so had the snow. We'd hardly had time for snowball fights, what with all the shoveling.

"Here she comes."

We hurried over to watch Mother put her suitcase into the back seat of our Model T. Mother wore her navy blue coat and wool hat. She was also wearing boots, a long woolen scarf, and gloves.

"You're not wearing your white dress," Jim said.

"No. I'll change into it for the demonstration."

"If it's this cold down there," I said, "you'll have to wear your winter things over it anyway."

Mother said, "No matter. They'll know we're suffragists by our signs and banners."

She had modeled the white dress with the purple and yellow banner for us when Dad was repairing the back wall of the barn. She also taught us the suffragist song to the tune of "My Country, 'Tis of Thee":

> Our country, now from thee,
> Claim we our liberty,
> In freedom's name.

It was catchy, but Jim and I were careful not to sing it around my father. It would have been like waving a red flag in front of a bad-tempered bull. Mother's large-brimmed white hat with the purple and gold flowers was, no doubt, in the hatbox she was now carefully placing beside her suitcase on the seat. She'll be sorry it doesn't have earflaps, I thought.

"Wish we were going," Jim said. "Are you really going to march, Mother?"

She patted his cheek. "Yes, dear," she said. "And we'll be marching down every street in America when we finally get the vote. Perhaps you boys will even march with me in Westfield when the thirty-sixth state has ratified."

I rolled my eyes at that. Parade down the main street of Westfield with a bunch of women? That would be the day.

"Are you going to march right into the White House?" Jim asked.

She shook her head. "They'd never allow that. President Wilson says he's for women's suffrage, but his heart's not in it —not the way Teddy Roosevelt's was. We'll march down Pennsylvania Avenue and up to the White House gates. President Wilson will know we're there, all right," she declared. "Some suffragists are going to chain themselves to the gates."

"Why?" Jim asked. "Why would they do a thing like that?"

"To make a statement," Mother said.

"Isn't a statement something you say?" Jim asked.

"Exactly," Mother said. She walked back into the house, ignoring Jim's puzzled look.

I smiled. I knew Mother would not be one of the women chaining herself to any fence, although some of the women in that group from Springfield might be silly enough to do it.

The campaign for women's rights had tamed down some during the fighting, but now that the Great War was over, Mother said it was full steam ahead on women's suffrage. She had a map on the wall behind her desk with each of the thirty-one states that had ratified the Nineteenth Amendment marked with a star. Votes were coming up in New Mexico and Oklahoma at the end of February.

After months of arguing, Congress had finally passed the amendment giving women the right to vote. Now it had to be ratified by thirty-six states, and that was by no means a sure thing, according to the newspaper articles my father muttered over. Lots of people were against it—even women, and that was beyond my mother's comprehension.

My father sputtered for a week when he heard that Mother actually planned to go to Washington. I don't think she'd told him yet that she had plans to go to all the New England states for demonstrations in the months ahead.

My father's arguments on the subject were always the same. If women were going to get the right to vote, it should be done with dignity. It would be a matter of debate among men and, eventually, become law if it was meant to be. Marches and demonstrations were unnecessary, Dad said, and disgraceful. Mother should restrict her activities in the matter to letter writing and even, he grudgingly allowed, debates.

As he said many times, he was a respectable farmer and citizen of Montgomery. What would people think of a man whose wife was parading through the streets? Fortunately, Washington was so far off, no one in Montgomery would hear about it.

I'd heard Dad tell Uncle Clint that he didn't really think that women ought to have the vote. It would coarsen women to become involved in politics, he said. I wasn't too sure what that meant, and he didn't say such things around Mother, of course. Talk about waving flags in front of a bull!

Dad came up from the barn.

"When will you be back, Grace?" he asked, keeping his eye on the Ford as if it might buck or bolt off any minute. He approached the automobile only when necessary and then with the caution he'd use around a jittery stallion.

"The march is tomorrow afternoon. I should be home a day or two after that," she said.

"Where will you stay?"

"They've found housing for all of us," she said.

"And you don't know where?" My father shook his head in amazement. "Why, Grace, heaven knows what sort of place you'll be sleeping in."

"I'll be with other suffragists, Fred."

"And you find that a comfort?"

"I'll be fine, Fred."

"And what about us? A woman belongs at home. 'The hand that rocks the cradle rules the world.'"

Mother grinned. "The hand that rocks the cradle belongs to a woman with a sore arm," she said. "Besides, dear, everyone in this family is long out of the cradle. You'll be fine. There's a pot of stew in the icebox that should do for tonight, and I've dressed a chicken for tomorrow. After that, you're on your own."

Dad looked even more dismayed, and so did we. The one thing my father ever cooked was tripe. He was the only one in the family who liked it, and Mother refused to cook it. Every so often, usually when Mother was away, Dad would dust tripe with flour, fry it in lard, and make a feast of the stuff. A few days with tripe on the menu would make skeletons of us all.

"Cheer up," Mother went on. "Winnie said she and Clint would stop by to make sure you're not starving to death."

We breathed a sigh of relief. Aunt Winnie was a super cook.

"What if that tarnatious machine runs out of gas, Grace?"

"I've plenty of gas, Fred. There are filling stations in Springfield, if I should need any more for the trip back."

"Well, you be careful down there, Grace. No telling what those suffragists will do next. Or the politicians either, especially the Democrats."

Mother gave him a peck on the cheek, hugged Jim and me, gave Rex a quick pat, and stepped up into the driver's seat.

She set the spark and opened the throttle, then reached across the seat for the crank. She grinned, holding out the crank to my father.

"Want to crank it for me, Fred?" she asked.

My father's look was enough; I took the crank. Dad watched as I cranked it a couple of times. He jumped back as the motor caught. I handed the crank back to Mother, and off she went in a blast of dust.

We were getting ready for bed the next night when the telephone rang. Four rings. It was for us.

My father, as always, refused to answer it. He hated the telephone almost as much as he hated motorcars. We were one of the first families in Montgomery to have one, at Mother's insistence. Dad had answered it once when it was three rings and, of course, three rings meant it was for the Jacksons. Dad hung up and never answered the telephone again.

So I was the one who got the news that Mother had been arrested.

YOKUM

My father had not reacted well to the news of Mother's arrest. I called Uncle Clint. By the time he and Aunt Winnie arrived, Dad had stopped shouting, which meant that Rex had stopped barking. Jim and I sat at the dining room table, pretending to do our homework. Dad was sitting in the Morris chair, muttering as he stared into the fire.

Aunt Winnie went straight to the kitchen and made toasted cheese sandwiches. Uncle Clint gave my father a shot of whiskey and took one himself.

"Washington! Bail her out," Dad muttered. "Trains! Who'll run the farm? Money! How much? Change in New Haven?"

"No, Dad," I said, "you don't have to change trains anywhere. You don't have to go to Washington. The suffragists have already posted bail for all those arrested. Mother said she'd just have to stay in Washington for the hearing next week."

Jim held up three fingers. I nodded. I had told Dad that

same thing three times before Uncle Clint arrived.

"Like a common criminal," Dad went on. "Thrown in with streetwalkers! Thieves!"

Aunt Winnie motioned me into the hall.

"Is she all right, Frank?" she asked.

I told her that Mother said it hadn't been bad, although the ride in the Black Maria was uncomfortable. They'd sung suffragist songs all the while and nearly driven the jailers crazy.

"Perhaps that's why they were only held a few hours," Aunt Winnie said. "Why did they arrest her? I thought marching was legal."

"I think it had something to do with chaining herself to the White House fence," I said.

Aunt Winnie glanced nervously over her shoulder at my father. "Does he know?" she asked.

❧

I think now, looking back on it, that Mother's arrest and the newspaper article about it that appeared on the front page of the local paper showing her in her chains had a lot to do with what came next, although I didn't connect it at the time.

One afternoon in February, Aunt Winnie and Uncle Clint came by. You could tell Aunt Winnie had been crying, but Uncle Clint seemed very excited.

They all sat in the parlor—Dad glancing nervously at Aunt Winnie as she blew her nose and tried not to snuffle. He sent

Jim and me out of the room. We ran upstairs. There was a register in the floor of the front hallway where sound as well as heat came up from downstairs. They must have thought we'd gone outside, because they didn't even bother to lower their voices. That was good; otherwise, you had to press your ear down on the register to hear what was said, and that hurt after a while.

By the time Jim and I got situated, Uncle Clint was talking. "The Stevens' lodge up in Becket—big place on Yokum Pond. They get folks, mostly war vets and businessmen, from New York, Hartford, and Boston, for fishing and hunting or just relaxing. Some just stay overnight. Others come for a week or more. They keep a bunch of horses, some saddle and some carriage. They do hayrides and the like."

"Darn fools!" Dad said. "Paying good money to stay way up there in the woods."

"They want us to run it," Uncle Clint said.

"Run it?" my mother said. "Why, you'd have to move up there."

We could hear Aunt Winnie crying now.

"Grace . . ." Dad began.

"And what do you know about running a lodge?" Mother interrupted. "There, there, Winnie."

"Well," Uncle Clint said, "I can hunt and catch a fish or two, and Winnie's a fair cook."

That got a rise out of Aunt Winnie. "Fair? I'm a good cook, and you know it, Clint."

"You certainly are a good cook, Winnie, but cooking for a lot of people isn't the same as cooking for just you and Clint," my mother said.

"That's true, Clint," Aunt Winnie said, seizing on Mother's words. "All those strangers to please." Her voice trembled.

"Who knows what those city folks will eat, anyway?" Dad added. "Who's running the place now?"

"Nobody," Uncle Clint said. "Family that was running it got wiped out in the flu epidemic last year. Died in a matter of days. Place has been closed since then. Now that the epidemic's over, Stevens wants it up and running. It was doing a good business until the influenza hit."

"How will you have time to care for the horses, Clint? Keeping up a stable of horses is a full-time job in itself. And there'd be upkeep. Keeping track of the expenses. What do you two know about running a business?" Mother asked.

"Not a darned thing," Uncle Clint said. "That's where you and Fred come in."

"Come in?" Dad said. "Grace and me? Oh, no. We're not coming in anywhere. If you and Winnie are fool enough to go traipsing up to Becket, more power to you. Leave us out of it."

"We can't do this if you won't come, Fred. Winnie and I— we need you and Grace and the boys as well. Grace, you ran that millinery shop before you married Fred. You've got a head for business. You can keep the books and manage things in the lodge, and Fred can take care of the horses. It'd be duck soup for you, Fred. The boys can help with chores. It's the big time, Fred."

"We can't even consider it," Mother said. "What would the boys do for school?"

"There's a nice little school right in Becket Center. Only about a three-mile stroll from the lodge," Uncle Clint said.

Jim and I looked at each other and rolled our eyes. Three miles is a long stroll to make twice a day in good weather. In the winter, it would be agony. It was twice as far from home as the school in Montgomery. Well, no matter. We knew Dad wasn't having any part of this deal.

"Don't plan on us," Dad repeated. "We're not going."

Jim and I smiled and nodded at each other.

"No, we can't possibly go," Mother said. "The suffragists have a meeting in Worcester next month. How would I ever get there or to any of the other meetings, for that matter, from way up in Becket? Even in the automobile, it would take all day. And I was planning to have an organizational meeting here in Montgomery next summer. Women around here need to become involved. I'm not building much interest with the pamphlets. I'll never get the women to go all the way to Becket."

Nobody said anything for a while. When my father spoke again, his voice sounded different.

"What kind of money are they talking about, Clint?"

We heard a gasp that must have come from Mother. Aunt Winnie bawled loudly.

"He'll pay us fifteen hundred, Fred, plus a bonus if we make a profit."

"Apiece?"

"Fifteen hundred for each family."

"For how long?"

"They close it down at Thanksgiving and don't open again until April," Uncle Clint said.

"Not even a full year, then. Fifteen hundred dollars plus a bonus, you say."

"Fred," said my mother. "You can't—"

"Plus free food and lodging." Uncle Clint broke right in. "That's free living, Fred."

"Free living," my father repeated.

"Yessir," Uncle Clint said.

"Fred!" Mother sounded desperate.

"You going to sell your place?" Dad asked, talking over her.

"Fred!" Mother protested again as Aunt Winnie continued to sob. "Clint!"

It was as if neither man heard.

"No, I'll rent it out," Uncle Clint said. "There's a family just come over from someplace in Europe. Rehor, their name is. Got three kids and looking for a place to farm. Nice folks, though they don't speak much English. They'll run my farm while they look for a place of their own. The salary from Stevens plus the rent from my place should do us fine. We'll have a nest egg when we're through. You and Grace could do well by it, Fred."

"I'd have to find someone—"

Mother gasped. "Fred," she said. "You can't."

But he could, and he did. Both Jim and I did our best to stop it. We pleaded. We said it would ruin our lives. We promised to do twice our chores and all of our homework every day. We promised everything we could think of to keep from leaving our friends, but we might as well have saved our breath.

Jim and I were sent out of the room night after night as Mother and Dad argued. We gave up listening through the register, but there was no doubt that my father won out. Turned out that the Rehors had some cousins who would take over our place, and before we knew it, we were packing for Becket.

Patch and Samson had to stay behind for the new folks, and we all spent some time saying sad goodbyes to them. Rex was nervously pacing from house to wagon as we loaded up. He must have been afraid he was being left behind, too. Dad had only to give a faint whistle when we were ready, and a much-relieved Rex leaped into the wagon, slathering Dad with kisses.

"Are you sure you want to take that thing all the way up there to the sticks?" Dad asked as Mother loaded up the Model T.

She put down the suitcases she was carrying. "Well, of course I'm going to take it, Fred," she said.

"Best leave it here," Dad said.

"Nonsense!" Mother declared. "We'll need it up there in Becket. We'll be miles from everything."

"What if you get a flat?" he asked.

"Then I'll fix it," she declared.

"Frank," my father said. "You ride with your mother."

I'd hoped that would happen. Maybe Mother would give me a chance to drive.

I cranked up the car when she set the spark. It caught first thing, and we chugged past as my father clicked the reins. I gave one backward glance at Montgomery as we turned toward Huntington and the way west.

We hadn't taken much with us. There was a good chunk of the Berkshire Mountains on the way to Becket, and Dad didn't want to tax Prince too much. We had some stuff in the back of the Ford, but Mother didn't want to overload it either. Uncle Clint said everything we needed was in the lodge, anyway. What we took with us was mostly clothes and things Mother called keepsakes—pictures and the like. And Mother made us take all our schoolbooks, of course.

As it was, the radiator overheated three times on the way up. We had to wait each time until it cooled, and add water from passing streams before we could go on. Fortunately the streams were full from melting snow.

Mother did let me drive through Huntington, but then the road began to curve too much as we climbed higher, and I was glad to turn the driving back to her.

Although it wasn't all that big, Mother's suffragist outfit was one of the things Dad said there just wasn't room for. Mother had nodded when he said it, but I could see the white skirt peeking out from a bundle in the Ford's back seat.

"It'll be all right, won't it, Mother?" I asked while we were waiting for the motor to cool.

"What? The car?"

"No, Becket. It'll be fun living with Aunt Winnie and Uncle Clint for a year, won't it?"

"You mean with Aunt Winnie, Uncle Clint, and a lodge full of men?" Mother asked. She touched the radiator with the tip of her finger and drew it back quickly. "Oh," she said, "things will work out. They usually do. But when women get the vote . . ."

Most of the snow in Montgomery was gone when we left, but we saw more and more snow on the ground as we climbed the hills toward Becket. It was a foot deep all around the lodge when we got there, but the drive was plowed. Even with all those stops, we'd beaten Dad and Jim.

For a few minutes, Mother and I just stared at the place that was to be our home. It was made of logs, and it was the biggest

building I'd ever seen. It made even our church, the biggest building in Montgomery, look tiny.

We were both half frozen. The Model T had a heater, but it sure didn't throw much heat. At least Dad and Jim had Rex and some blankets for warmth. We just had a couple of lap robes.

There were two entrances to the lodge. One was obviously the main one—a big wooden sign hung over the carved wooden doors, with yellow letters: YOU COME TO YOKUM— WELCOME. Right in front of us was a smaller back door. All the doors were locked.

"Hmmph!" Mother said. "Welcome indeed! Well, no point in just standing here. We'll freeze to death. Let's get unloaded."

So Mother and I bustled around unloading the car and piling stuff up by the back door. Fortunately, Uncle Clint and Aunt Winnie pulled in soon after we were done.

Mother hugged Aunt Winnie, who was crying.

"Oh, Grace," she sobbed. "What have they done to us?" She looked around her, waving her arms. "Woods!" she cried. "Nothing but woods all around us. Probably full of mean bears and angry tigers."

"Um, I don't think there are any tigers in the woods, Aunt Winnie," I said.

"How do you know?" she asked as she brushed by me. "You just got here." Uncle Clint smiled and shook his head.

Uncle Clint hustled to unlock the back door, and we stepped

into a tiny room with hooks and shelves on all sides filled with all sorts of clothing: hats, coats, mittens, bathing suits, boots, and shoes.

"Whose are these?" I asked.

Uncle Clint said, "They're spares for anybody who needs them. Half the guests come unprepared for the weather, Mr. Stevens said. Have to keep everything in all sizes handy. If there's anything there you want, help yourself."

After a quick glance to make sure Mother wasn't looking, I grabbed a pair of mittens with long cuffs. There'd probably be no other kids around to make fun of me, but I wouldn't wear them to school, just in case.

"Come on, Frank," Uncle Clint said. "Let's leave the women to their tears and get a fire going."

I took a look around as we went through the kitchen. A gigantic black stove took up one side. The stovepipe bent twice before it entered the wall up near the high ceiling. A long table went down the middle of the room, with shelves underneath stacked with white dishes of all sorts. Pots and pans dangled from hooks above the table. There was a soapstone sink with a pump, just like the one at home, and a big white icebox on the other side of the kitchen.

Heat from that stove sure felt good, and I would have lingered there but Uncle Clint motioned me on. A swinging door led into the main room, where it was almost as cold as outdoors.

I thought the kitchen was big, but this room put it to shame.

It was big enough to fit the whole population of Montgomery, and maybe Wyben as well. A fieldstone fireplace covered most of one wall. The room was two stories tall and peaked in the center, with twelve large beams a foot or more wide going from front to back. Three big chandeliers hung down along the peak. There were couches and chairs and tables all over the place and a big organ against the inside wall. Antlered deer heads stuck out of the wall above us, staring down with glassy eyes. One head hung on each side of the fireplace, and two more stared down from the railed balcony that went around halfway up one side of the room. The place smelled musty and damp. I thought about our cozy parlor back in Montgomery, where strangers were sitting now.

"You going to stand there gawking much longer, or shall we get a fire going?" Uncle Clint asked. "There's split logs on the porch. Start with the small ones. I've got paper and kindling here." He knelt by the fireplace and I hustled to get the wood. Glass doors opened onto a screened-in porch that went across the front of the place on the pond side. Snow had blown in through the screens.

By the time Dad, Jim, and Rex arrived, things were warming up, although no one wanted to be very far from the fireplace. Aunt Winnie had brought soup and had it simmering on the stove. We made short work of that. With our bellies full, Jim and I bundled up to take a look around outside.

The lodge faced the water, and it took a while just to walk

around it to the front. There was a big outhouse at the edge of the clearing—a four-seater. Jim and I christened it.

The land slanted down to the pond, so what had been the first floor was now over our heads. The cellar had windows looking out on the pond. Around us were the pilings supporting the porch. The cellar door was locked, but peeking through the windows, we could see canoes and a rowboat upside down on sawhorses. Jim and I gave each other the thumbs up. This place might have its good points, after all. Then we turned to the pond. It was covered with ice, and Rex was already running in circles on it.

"Jimminey!" Jim said. "It's not a pond. It's a lake."

It was good-sized, and there was nothing on it but the lodge and its outbuildings. We couldn't hear a sound except for the occasional cawing of crows. Huge trees were everywhere— mostly pine, chestnut, and oak.

Even though our breath was freezing in front of our faces, Jim and I looked across the snow-covered ice and talked about the swimming and the fishing we'd do next summer.

"Now, here's our boys!" Uncle Clint exclaimed when we came back inside, as if he hadn't seen us for years. "How do you like your new home?" That sent Aunt Winnie into more tears.

"See to Winnie, Grace," Dad said as he motioned us to join him and hurried out the door.

"Where are all the people?" Jim asked, pulling out a wooden box from the stack in the wagon.

"Nobody's coming until the first week of April," Dad said. "We've got time to get settled first."

"Maybe Aunt Winnie will have stopped crying by then," I said.

"Hmmmph!" was my father's answer to that.

We had a little trouble when Dad slammed the back door as we came back inside. The vibration caused the stovepipe to fall with a loud crash, covering everything and everybody with soot.

The noise brought the others running. Mother, Aunt Winnie, and Jim and I cleaned up the kitchen while my father and Uncle Clint worked at reattaching the stovepipe.

"Now," Dad said when they had finished, "you boys be careful next time not to slam the door, or that thing will fall again."

"It wasn't us," Jim protested, but no one seemed to care.

Finally, we all went back into the main room. There were three sets of glass doors that led out onto the porch to the left of the fireplace wall. The walls were knotty pine, and there were big bay windows on either side of the front door.

The part of the room nearest the kitchen was set up as a dining room. There was a great long table with chairs all around it. Extra leaves for the table and more chairs were up against the near wall. It looked like it could seat about twenty people.

"Poor Aunt Winnie," Jim said, "having to cook for all those people."

"Poor us," I said, "having to do all those dishes."

"Us?" Jim cried.

"Who else?" I said with a shrug.

That was such a sad thought that we just stood there for a minute. Then we ran up the stairs to the balcony. The heat hadn't reached up here yet, and it smelled kind of bad. We were eye to eye with the deer heads, and that was a little creepy, so we turned our attention to the rooms. We raced down the hall, throwing open doors, one right after the other. We counted twelve bedrooms. Some of them were large, with two or three beds; others had only one bed and a chest of drawers. Each room had a basin and pitcher on a stand under the window, with a chamber pot under each bed, of course.

We each chose a big room with a large bed for our own and threw our coats and hats inside. All the adults were still standing by the fire when we came down.

Uncle Clint said, "Boys, your room is down that hall there, right beside ours, next to the laundry room. Your mother and father will be across the hall."

"That's all right," I said. "We picked out rooms upstairs."

"Sorry." Uncle Clint shook his head. "Those are all for guests up there. We hired help get rooms down here—unless, of course, you boys plan to be paying guests."

We retrieved our things from the upstairs bedrooms and found the bunk beds in a small room at the end of the downstairs hall. Back in Montgomery, we each had our own bedrooms. Now we'd have to share this tiny one. I got dibs on the top bunk.

We peeked into the laundry room, which had two washing machines and two wringers attached to a deep sink. It smelled of soap. The next room was set up for an office.

"However will we manage?" Aunt Winnie was saying when Jim and I went back to the main room. "It's so big. The cooking . . . the cleaning . . . all those beds. Why, the laundry alone will take us all day."

"You'll have some help," Uncle Clint said.

"You bet we will," Mother said. "If you think you men are going to—"

"No, no. I mean besides us," he said. "There's a staff of three, two girls and a handyman."

"Do they do the dishes?" Jim asked.

"When we have a crowd, they will," Uncle Clint said.

"How big's a crowd?" Jim asked.

"More than twelve guests," Dad said. "Otherwise the dishwashing is yours, boys."

"Do they empty the chamber pots?" I asked.

Uncle Clint smiled and nodded. "For the guests," he said. "Otherwise, it's every man for himself." Jim and I sent out a simultaneous sigh of relief.

"Are more than twelve coming first?" I asked.

"Afraid not, fellas," Uncle Clint said. "Only five."

"We can't make much of a profit with only five guests at a time," Mother said. "How far ahead are we booked?"

"Don't know for sure," Uncle Clint said. "Stevens is supposed to send us the schedule."

"Where does he advertise?" Mother asked.

"Boston and New York newspapers," Uncle Clint answered.

"Does the help's pay come out of our fifteen hundred?" Dad asked. "Because we can manage without—"

"Nope," Uncle Clint said, cutting off Mother's protest. "They're on the payroll."

"Do they live here?" Mother asked.

"No," said Uncle Clint. "The maids—Rose and Martha Moore—are sisters. They live in the village. They worked in the mill for a while and got laid off. They worked here last year and somehow survived the flu. They come every morning, do the laundry, change the beds, and clean the guest rooms."

"And do the dishes when there's more than twelve people," Jim reminded him.

Uncle Clint nodded and went on. "They're hard workers. They come at eight every morning and stay until the work's done, usually about seven. You just need to feed them at noon, Winnie."

Aunt Winnie shook her head. "We'll feed them supper too, Clint, when they stay late. It's only fair."

He smiled. "Okay with me."

"That's a lot of work with just those girls for help," Mother said. "If we have twelve guests or more . . ."

"There's several girls in the village who'd like the extra work," Uncle Clint said. "The mills aren't hiring now. We'll use them if we need to."

"You said there was a hired man," Dad said.

"Yeah. Name's Rooshy." Uncle Clint grinned.

"Is that his first name or his last name?" Jim asked.

Uncle Clint shrugged. "Beats me. He's not the most ambitious man I ever saw. He lives in what used to be a guest cabin down by the lake. He'll take most of his meals with us. He's got just one tooth, right in the front. He chews and spits, but he's all we've got."

"How does he chew with just one tooth?" Jim asked. "Don't you need two teeth for that?"

"Beats me," Uncle Clint said. "He seems to have no trouble eating. It's working that he seems to have some trouble with."

"What does he do here? Besides chew and spit," my father wanted to know.

"I haven't actually caught him doing anything yet. Shovels out, mows, I would think. He must have started the wood fire in the kitchen stove and plowed the drive before we got here. It snowed last night."

"Let's see the horses," Dad said, "and find that no-account Rooshy."

FIRST GUESTS

"Do you think Samson and Patch are okay, Frank?"

"Yeah," I said. "They'll be fine."

"Do you think they miss us?"

"Maybe."

"Do you miss them, Frank?"

"Nah," I said, but of course I did. I missed the horses; I missed my friends and I even missed school, but there was so much work to do those first weeks at the lodge that we hardly had time to mope.

Even with just our family and Uncle Clint and Aunt Winnie, Rose, Martha, and Rooshy, there were lots of dishes at every meal. We didn't like to imagine what it would be like with more guests.

The good news was that Mother said they wouldn't have time to get us enrolled in the new school until April. You know how bad we felt about that, but she made us do problems from our arithmetic books every night.

Whenever they gave us a chance, Jim and I explored. We hiked all the way around the lake. There was still a lot of snow back in the woods, and we didn't dare walk on the ice after we heard crackling when we stepped on it. There were places where a terrific fort could be built, but they didn't give us time enough for that. Jim spotted a place halfway up the mountain that he thought might be a cave, but getting up there would have to wait.

Rose and Martha may have thought that the lodge was clean before we got there, but they hadn't seen it through my mother's eyes. Every room, including the kitchen, had to be completely emptied out and scrubbed from floor to ceiling, and all the dishes and pans had to be washed, all the linens boiled, before things passed my mother's inspection. We all went to bed exhausted every night, but the lodge smelled of furniture polish and soap now.

The kitchen gave the most trouble. Seemed like we'd just get everything in there cleaned up and Dad would slam the back door again. Funny how it happened no matter how many times he warned us to be careful, and it was amazing how much soot could build up in that thing in just a few days.

Jim and I had a good time with Rooshy.

"Do we call you Rooshy or Mr. . . .?" I asked when we met him.

"Yeah, that'll be fine," he said.

"Which?" Jim asked.

"Yup," he said, ignoring Jim's confused look.

Rooshy may not have been much of a hand for work, but he loved to talk. How he managed to talk with that huge chaw of tobacco in his mouth all the time I never could figure out. He told us there was a soapstone ledge halfway up a hill near us where you could see bowls Indians had chipped out and an Indian rock shelter over by an abandoned emery mine. He said there was a haunted house down the road where Old Man Barnes had hung himself years ago and could still be seen late at night roaming the house and the woods near it.

Jim's eyes got wide when he heard that. "Jimminey!" he whispered.

"Rooshy," my mother warned. "Don't scare the children."

Aunt Winnie placed a spittoon on the floor beside him.

"Will you take us there?" I asked.

"Why, sure," Rooshy said. He pushed the spittoon to one side with his foot, went to the door, and spit a large stream of tobacco juice onto the snow bank. "If your father lays off a bit and I get a chance to catch up on my sleep," he said.

Mother examined the account books and said they were in deplorable shape. She announced that it would take her months just to figure out whether we had a thriving enterprise or a bankrupt business going here.

Aunt Winnie tried out a different supper on us each night,

doubling, tripling, and quadrupling her recipes. My father watched Aunt Winnie, and Aunt Winnie watched us as we tasted the food. It was touch and go. Some of those recipes seemed to multiply better than others, and it was hard for us not to show it when something didn't come out right. Aunt Winnie would sit there, biting her lip as we took a careful first taste. If we took another right away, things would settle down. My father and Aunt Winnie would relax, and we'd all enjoy the meal. If the new recipe was bad, and we pushed the food around on our plates a bit or made even the slightest face, Aunt Winnie would burst into tears and rush from the room.

Dad would sigh and say, "Grace, see to Winnie."

After she got Aunt Winnie calmed down, Mother would help her remove that food and rustle up some leftovers from a more successful meal, but that, of course, meant more dishes.

By the end of the week, Aunt Winnie had four meals that we'd all agreed were good enough to serve to any guest, and times around the supper table got better. Oatmeal, eggs, pancakes, and steak or bacon worked well for breakfast, and dinner at noon was usually stew or soup and bread. We hoped no guest would stay more than four days for supper, or there might be a problem.

My father had carefully inspected each of the lodge's horses and pronounced them fit enough, although I think Prince had reservations about a couple of them. Dad was disgusted with the condition of the stables and announced they'd have to be scrubbed down thoroughly before the week was out. Uncle Clint got pretty good at finding Rooshy.

"I was just looking for my hammer," Rooshy would say as Uncle Clint brought him to my father.

"Easier to do that with your eyes open and by looking in the tool shed," Dad declared.

There were four hunting dogs in pens at the back of the stables. Rex had greeted each one and they seemed to pass his inspection. Uncle Clint said the only test of a good hunting dog was whether or not it would hunt, so he and Rooshy and the dogs spent a lot of time together in the woods. They only brought back a couple of grouse, but I don't know how much of that was the dogs' fault.

Rooshy did a lot of complaining as well as chewing and spitting, but by Friday morning my father announced that things at the stable would do. He wouldn't let anyone else work on the horses. Rooshy said he was sorry to hear that, but it didn't sound as if he meant it.

My father hitched a matched team of horses to the surrey one Friday afternoon at the beginning of April. You could hear Prince whinny in protest at being left behind as Dad and Uncle Clint left the yard. Jim and I knew how Prince felt. They were going down to the railroad depot in Becket Center to pick up our first guests. We had loaded them up with blankets and Thermos bottles full of hot coffee and whiskey.

Aunt Winnie was a wreck. "What if they don't like fried

chicken?" she fretted as she stirred things in the pots and lifted stove lids to check the fire over and over again.

"Don't be ridiculous, Winnie," my mother said. "Everybody likes fried chicken, and yours is the best I've ever tasted. And the rolls have risen beautifully. Your dumplings are second to none, and you've got beets, carrots, and turnips enough in those pots to feed an army. No one's going hungry tonight."

By the time Rex barked and tore off down the road to meet the wagon, we were all as nervous as Aunt Winnie. Jim and I hung back as they drove in, but Dad hollered for us to come help with the luggage. He was still hollering for Rooshy when we'd brought the last of the luggage inside.

Lordy, what a lot of luggage there was. There were five men and they were only staying three days, but they had so many bags, Uncle Clint had to go back to the depot for a second load.

It took my father, Rose, Martha, Jim, and me two trips upstairs, and we had just got all the bags into the guest rooms when Uncle Clint was back with the next load and we had to start all over again.

Rooshy showed up just as we'd finished. "Gosh," he said. "Wish you'd called me to help with that."

Fortunately for Rooshy the guests were coming downstairs, so my father had to bite back his words. Mother made the introductions. Two of the men, Mr. Greenberg and Mr. Allen, were bankers from New York and appeared to be good friends. Mr. Jacobs and Mr. Healy were railroad men and also knew each other.

The fifth man, Mr. Snow, was the odd man out, but that didn't seem to bother him a bit. It didn't take long to figure out why most of that luggage ended up in Mr. Snow's room. He came down in a red velvet smoking jacket, ascot tie, and black trousers that looked like velvet. Since the other men wore flannel shirts and regular trousers, Mr. Snow caught quite a bit of our attention.

Mother had hold of both Jim and me by the shoulder and her foot on top of Rooshy's left foot, so nobody said anything about the outfit and we all started in to eating. How Mr. Snow managed to put away so much food I couldn't figure out, because it seemed to me that he talked nonstop all through supper.

He'd been to deepest Africa and South America and lots of places I'd never heard of. He'd shot elephants and lions and other fierce beasts even as they charged toward him—stopped them with a single bullet right between the eyes. He said he wouldn't even bother with something as small as our deer heads.

Jim said, "Well, they're already dead. Nobody would want to shoot a dead deer head, would they?"

Mr. Snow gave Jim a quick glance and went right on.

He'd met just about every important person you ever heard of and was best friends with several. Apparently he and Teddy

Roosevelt had grown up together, and Mr. Snow had advised him about several government matters while he was in office. Jim's mouth was wide open whenever it wasn't full of food, but by the end of the meal even Jim seemed to have some trouble believing the man.

When Mr. Snow finally drew a breath, Uncle Clint told them all about the riding, the hunting and fishing, and other activities that were available. He asked the men what they were interested in doing.

Mr. Greenberg and Mr. Allen both said they were looking to relax. Mr. Greenberg declared that the most physical activity he was interested in was a game of chess or cribbage and maybe turning the pages of a book after he'd napped a bit. Mr. Allen said that if Aunt Winnie continued to cook as well as this, he might just stay right at the table and wait for the next meal. You should have seen Aunt Winnie's smile then.

Mr. Healy and Mr. Jacobs had brought some papers with them and said they were looking for a quiet place to work tomorrow, and then maybe on Sunday they'd go for a walk if it got a bit warmer.

Mr. Snow was shocked that the others were going to just laze around. He said he wanted to go hunting as soon as possible. He asked where the hunting guide was.

Uncle Clint said, "You're talking to him."

Mr. Snow looked him up and down. He appeared a bit doubtful but said, "Well, let's go!"

"Now?" Uncle Clint said. "There's nothing to hunt at night except raccoons."

"Nonsense!" Mr. Snow declared. "There's deer and bear out in those woods, and who knows what else."

"Well," Uncle Clint said. "The bears and the deer may be there, but it's illegal to shoot them at night."

"Who's to catch us?" Mr. Snow said. "You're not a game warden, are you?"

"No," Uncle Clint said, "but I have two rules about hunting. You shoot only what's legal, and you eat anything you shoot."

"Coons, huh?" Mr. Snow said. "Nothing but coons?"

"Right," Uncle Clint said.

That silenced Mr. Snow, and Uncle Clint sat down by the fire and started unlacing his shoes. Mother, Aunt Winnie, Jim, and I began clearing the table. Rooshy usually left for his cabin right after supper, but he sat down in one of the chairs nearest the fire and nodded off. Dad picked up the newspaper.

The guests also settled down in front of the fire.

Then Mr. Snow said, "All right. We'll go coon hunting."

"Ever eat raccoon?" Uncle Clint asked without looking up from the knot he was working on.

"No, but they're edible, aren't they?"

"If you're hungry enough, most anything is," Rooshy said, opening his eyes just a tad.

"Do you know how to cook raccoon?" Mr. Snow asked Aunt Winnie.

"Winnie can make anything taste good." Uncle Clint spoke up before she could answer. "I guarantee you, she'll cook as many as you shoot."

Aunt Winnie put down a dish and grabbed for Mother's hand.

"Then let's go," Mr. Snow said. "Any of you others coming?"

The other guests quickly refused.

"Too bad then. Back in a jiff," Mr. Snow said, and he went upstairs.

"Dang fool," Dad declared, looking over his open newspaper.

"Shhh!" Mother said. "He'll hear you."

"I don't know how to cook raccoon," Aunt Winnie whispered.

"I don't think you need to worry about that," Uncle Clint said.

"Pshaw!" Dad said. "Never heard such lies." He rattled his newspaper. "Teddy Roosevelt's best buddy? Big-game hunter, my foot. I'd like to see him get his comeuppance."

"Now," Rooshy said. "Now that's an interesting prospect. Right interesting." He went to the back door and spit.

Uncle Clint was grinning as he relaced his high-top shoes and grabbed a jacket.

"Shucks," he said. "It's going to be a great night with a big-game hunter like that along. You coming, Fred?"

Dad said, "I think I'll leave this to you and Rooshy."

"You boys want to join us?" Uncle Clint asked. "Watch a big-game hunter show his skills?"

Mother started to protest.

"They might learn something," Rooshy said. "Shucks! Maybe Snow knew Lincoln. You can never tell what education the night might hold."

"Nothing dangerous," Mother warned.

"Nah," Rooshy said. "There's nothing dangerous out there except for the ghost of Old Man Barnes."

"Jimminey!" Jim said.

Mother sighed and said, "Go ahead, boys. But dress warm."

"It's April," I protested.

"It's the first of April in the mountains, and it's night," Mother said firmly. "Dress warm and be careful."

"If you see the ghost," Dad said, "give him my regards."

"How do you do that?" Jim asked me as we went to get our coats.

"Do what?" I asked, reaching for a hat.

"Give a ghost your regards."

"I think a handshake will do," I said.

Jim was still mulling over that when Mr. Snow came back down.

Dad raised his eyebrows, but Uncle Clint and Rooshy's faces were totally without expression. Jim and I were much impressed, and I'm sure our faces showed it. Mr. Snow had on a bright red and black jacket with big red leather gloves. A hat like the one Sherlock Holmes wore sat on his head, with the flaps down over his ears. His black trousers had leather patches on the knees. His boots were highly polished. Mr. Snow pointed to each item and told us how much he had paid for it at Abercrombie and Fitch in New York City. Even with my head for ciphering, it added up to thousands.

He had two of the shiniest, biggest shotguns I ever saw. He said one was a George Worthington double barrel and the other was a Churchill Limited.

Jim thought he said "George Washington" and wanted to know if he'd used them in the Revolution.

"Worthington, not Washington," Mr. Snow said. "Do the children have to come?"

"You going to shoot two guns at a time?" Rooshy asked, ignoring his question.

"Of course not," Mr. Snow said.

"Then put one of those things down before you hurt someone," Uncle Clint said.

"Won't you need a gun?" Mr. Snow asked.

"No," Uncle Clint said. "We don't want to shoot too many coons. Leave some for the next fella."

"What about you, Rooshy? Want to use this?" Mr. Snow held the gun toward him.

"Oh, no. Wouldn't know how to handle anything that fancy." Rooshy backed away, holding his hands up. "I don't usually use a gun for coons. I just leap on them and strangle them from behind."

Mr. Snow gave him a doubtful look.

"Wow!" Jim said. "Will you do that tonight, Rooshy?"

"Nah," Rooshy said. "I'm just a guide tonight. Don't want to steal Mr. Snow's thunder."

He took down the lantern and lit it. Rex pulled himself away from the front of the fireplace, and we all went down to the dog pens.

The dogs began to bark and jump all over the place when they realized we were going hunting. Uncle Clint opened the door, and they streamed out of the pens like water over the falls and headed off into the woods. Rex chased after them for a bit and then seemed to lose heart. He came back to walk with us. We could hear the hounds yapping as they ran far ahead. In just a few minutes, they began to bay. That got Rex running again, and he soon left us behind.

"Sounds like they've treed something," Uncle Clint said.

"Hope it's a bear. Hurry up. What are you waiting for?" Mr. Snow said, and he ran off in the direction of the sound. His gun fired as he fell.

Uncle Clint helped him up. "Take the shells out of that thing," he said.

"No," Mr. Snow said, brushing himself off. "It'll be all right."

"You're apt to shoot someone I'm fond of," Uncle

Clint said. "Give me the shells."

Nobody moved while Mr. Snow stared at Uncle Clint. Finally he said, "Oh, all right." He broke open the gun, took the shells from the chamber, and gave them to Uncle Clint. "But be sure you get them to me in a hurry when I need them." Then we set off again.

The dogs were baying and circling a tall pine tree that stood on the edge of a steep ravine. The tree had no low branches; the first ones were up about twenty feet. When Rooshy tilted the lantern a bit, it caught the glow of two bright eyes in those branches.

"Is it a bear?" Mr. Snow asked.

"No," Uncle Clint said patiently. "Eyes are too close together for a bear. It's a coon."

Mr. Snow held out his hand. "Quick," he said. "Give me the shells."

"Stand back, boys," Uncle Clint said, handing him the shells.

Mr. Snow quickly loaded his gun and knelt to aim it straight up. He'd have fired if Uncle Clint hadn't stayed his hand.

"Can you see it?" he asked. "Can you see what you're shooting at?"

"Not right this minute," Mr. Snow said. "But we saw the eyes a minute ago."

"If you can't see it, you can't shoot it," Uncle Clint said.

"Another rule?" Mr. Snow sighed as he stood up.

"Yessir," Uncle Clint said.

"What do we do then?" Mr. Snow asked.

"Well," Rooshy said, "seems like we've got a couple of choices here. We can wait until the coon gets hungry and comes down on its own, or we can go get the coon."

"We can't wait," Mr. Snow said. "It may take days for the coon to get that hungry."

"True," Rooshy said. "And he probably won't accept our kind invitation to come down. You'll just have to shinny on up that tree and shake it down."

"Shinny?" Mr. Snow asked nervously. "Can't you do that?"

"Well, sure," Rooshy said, "but that wouldn't be fair to you. You want to hunt coon, why then, shaking it down is the most fun part."

"You can shinny, can't you?" Uncle Clint asked. "Big-game hunter like you must have shinnied up palm trees and redwood trees and goodness knows what else."

"Well, of course, I have," Mr. Snow said. "I'm just not sure how to shinny up a pine tree."

"Show him how, Jim," Uncle Clint said.

Jim nodded and clasped the trunk with his arms and knees and began to shinny up the tree. Jim was halfway up the trunk when Uncle Clint said, "That's enough. Come on back down, Jim. You'll be in Mr. Snow's way."

"You see how?" Uncle Clint asked Mr. Snow as Jim scrambled back down.

"Yes, of course. Nothing to it. But won't the coon just run

away before I can get up there? The boy may have already scared it away."

"Run?" Uncle Clint asked. "Run where? There's no place for it to go but down here. If it does that, the dogs will catch it for you." He shone the lantern up into the branches again, and there were those gleaming eyes.

Uncle Clint cupped his hands near the trunk of the pine and said, "Put your foot here, and I'll boost you up a bit."

"Boost me up?"

Rooshy said, "That's the way, Clint. Give him a bit of a start. That's the thing to do. Give me your gun first."

"Won't I need it up there?" Mr. Snow asked.

"Oh," Rooshy said. "I didn't realize you could shinny with just one arm. Should have known. Sure. You hold on to it."

"Well," Mr. Snow said, handing the gun to Rooshy, "perhaps I'd better not, this one time." He put his right foot into Uncle Clint's cupped hands. He grasped the trunk of the tree as Uncle Clint gave a shove, and there was Mr. Snow holding onto the tree trunk for dear life.

"What do I do?" he asked, his voice tight with the strain.

"Shinny on up," Uncle Clint said. He put both hands under Mr. Snow's bottom and said, "Just like Jim showed you. I'll count. When I get to three and shove, you move your arms up higher and sort of walk up the trunk with your knees. Ready?"

"I . . . guess . . . so," Mr. Snow said.

"One, two, *three!*" Uncle Clint said. He shoved, and Mr.

Snow moved. That is, he moved his arms and his knees, but it didn't look like he made much progress on the trunk.

"That's the way!" Uncle Clint called. "You're doing fine. Keep at it."

Rooshy handed the lantern to Uncle Clint and pointed down into the ravine, holding a finger to his lips.

Uncle Clint nodded and began to sidle slowly down into the ravine, motioning Jim and me to join him.

Rooshy spit some tobacco juice down by the trunk and leaned against the tree.

"This is a very hard tree to climb," Mr. Snow said. "Hard to get much purchase on. Doesn't feel like I'm getting anywhere."

Rooshy said nothing, but Uncle Clint called, "You're doing fine. Just look down for a minute, if heights don't bother you."

The woods were dark as pitch, so all Mr. Snow could see was the lantern we were holding, and we were quite a way down in the ravine by then.

"Right!" Mr. Snow said. He was puffing pretty hard. "Didn't realize how far I'd come. I must be nearly at those branches."

"Almost," Uncle Clint called up. "Keep at it."

"How long before you tell him that he's only a couple of feet off the ground, Uncle Clint?" I asked softly.

"Depends on how long it takes to let some of that hot air out," he whispered back. "Hard to tell with a man like Snow. Let's give him a few more minutes."

A little while later Mr. Snow called down. "I don't think I can hold on much longer. I didn't realize those branches were this far up. I'm getting very tired."

"Don't quit now," Uncle Clint hollered back. "You're nearly there. Can't you feel the coon's breath? Get ready to shake him down."

"Oh, right!" Mr. Snow gasped. "I can hear it breathing now."

"I thought so," Uncle Clint yelled. "Keep at it now."

We were crouched at the bottom of the ravine when Mr. Snow called, "Help me! I can't hold on any longer! I'm going to fall. One of you climb up here and help me."

"Better put your feet down," Rooshy said as we began climbing back up the ravine.

"My . . . my feet down?" Mr. Snow said. He didn't appear to notice that Rooshy's voice was coming from right behind him. "You mean let go of the tree with my knees?"

"Yep."

"Won't that make me fall?"

"Put your feet down," Rooshy repeated.

We were all back up to the tree trunk when Mr. Snow very cautiously put first one foot and then the other down on firm ground. It was a quiet walk home.

THE WOODPILE

Mother decided that we needed to improve the bookings at the lodge if we were going to make a go of it, so she designed some brochures and brought us all together for judgment on the mockup.

"You Come to Yokum," it said on the cover. "A beautiful lodge deep in the Berkshire Mountains, featuring excellent food, beautiful scenery, in restful surroundings. Swimming, boating, hiking, horseback riding available."

"Very nice, but it needs photographs," Uncle Clint said. "Something to show off the place."

"Right," Dad said. "Take a picture of the lodge, Grace. You're the photographer."

"All right," Mother said. "I'll use some views of the lodge and the lake, but for the front, I think we need a picture of Winnie."

"Me?" Aunt Winnie gasped. "Oh, Grace. Not me. Take a picture of the boys."

"Somehow," Mother said, "I don't think business men would

be attracted to a picture of Jim and Frank, handsome specimens though they are."

"Then take a picture of Clint and Fred."

"I'm the designer of this brochure and the business sense in this thing, if we can call it a business," Mother stated, "and it's you on the cover, Winnie. Let's see. Where to have you? I know. In the rowboat."

"Heavens! Not in a boat. I can't swim," Aunt Winnie said, wiping her hands on her apron. "I'm afraid of the water."

"The boat will be tied to the dock. You won't drown unless you leap out of it," Mother said.

"Are you sure? What if it sinks?"

"Then I shall jump in and save you," Uncle Clint said.

"Well, all right. Then let me get cleaned up a bit."

When we got the brochures a few weeks later, there was the boat with Aunt Winnie, under the words "You Come to Yokum." She was holding onto the oars a little awkwardly and looked anything but confident, but Uncle Clint said she looked like a tried and true sailor of the seven seas.

❧

Mother drove us down to the village school the following Monday. It was smaller than the one in Montgomery, but not by much. The teacher turned out to be a skinny little woman at least half a head shorter than I. Her name was Miss Drysdale. Turned out the kids called her Miss Dried-up, but not to her face. Jim and I had never had a woman teacher before and we weren't sure what to make of her, but she looked to be easier to manage than Mr. Stanwyck back in Montgomery.

Miss Drysdale had her hands on our shoulders as she took us into the classroom and introduced us. "Boys and girls," she said. "We have new students today, James and Franklin Carlyle. Say 'Good morning and welcome,' class."

I winced. Nobody ever called us that.

The class stood and said, "Good morning and welcome, James and Franklin."

Miss Drysdale smiled. "Very nice, class. Now James and Franklin, say 'Good morning, class.'"

Jim and I sort of mumbled something.

"Now, boys," she said. "That won't do. We speak up clearly here. Lift your heads. Look directly at the class, and let's hear that again."

I glanced at Jim, and I'm sure my face was as red as his as we looked at the class. Some of the kids were grinning. We knew and they knew there was trouble in store.

Miss Drysdale squeezed our shoulders a little harder, and we said, "Good morning, class."

"I'm sure you're all going to be good friends with your new classmates. James, you sit in the fourth row with the other fourth-graders, and Franklin, you'll join the sixth-graders."

Jim and I gave a doubtful glance at each other and sat down.

I say "sat," but since none of the sixth-graders budged an inch, it was more of a crouch for me, with one cheek on the bench and the other suspended into the aisle. There was one girl at the far end of the bench with her nose in a book who didn't even turn to look at me. The three sixth-grade boys made up for it though, by staring at me with no expression on their faces whatsoever. I looked over at Jim, who was getting similar looks from the boys on his bench.

After the pledge and the prayer, Miss Drysdale handed out the seatwork and then began calling each grade to recite at the front of the room, starting with the first-graders. I kept my eyes on my papers even though they weren't hard, and I could have finished them in no time. I spent most of the morning remembering the new kids that came to school in Montgomery and what we'd put them through.

Recess worked just about as I suspected it would. I followed my row into the cloakroom, but my jacket and boots weren't where I'd put them. My lunch pail was open and empty. Jim had the same trouble and, by the time we'd fished our coats out of the waste barrel and put them on, the others were all outside. We took about four steps onto the playground before we were surrounded.

The fight didn't really amount to much. There wasn't time for anyone to draw blood before Miss Drysdale was there to break it up. How she decided which kids to hold back, I don't know, but I was still wiping the mud from my knees when she had one of the sixth-grade boys, one of the fourth-grade boys, and Jim all lined up against the building. She motioned to me to join them.

"Roger Ferris," she said, addressing the sixth-grader. "We have spoken about this before. You assured me it would not happen again."

"Well, he started it!" Roger said.

"Roger?"

"Sorry, Miss Drysdale," he muttered, head down.

"Head up, Roger," Miss Drysdale said. "Head up and look at me. Speak distinctly. What have you to say, Roger?"

Roger brought his head up. "I'm sorry, Miss Drysdale."

"And you, Michael Russell," she went on. "What have you to say for yourself?"

"I'm sorry, Miss Drysdale," said the boy from Jim's bench.

"And you two," she said, turning her attention to Jim and me. "What a way is this to begin a new school?"

"Sorry, Miss Drysdale," Jim and I said in unison. There was no way we were going to tell her it wasn't our fight to start.

She pointed to a woodpile out by the edge of the playground.

"I want that cord of wood brought here, right next to the building," she said, indicating a spot to the left of the door. "And I want it stacked neatly."

"What about lunch?" Michael asked.

"Time for that when the work is done," she said.

Since neither Jim nor I had lunches waiting, this didn't matter much to us.

Miss Drysdale walked back into the schoolhouse and, after a minute spent swearing softly at each other, all four of us started to work. Roger managed to hit me in the hip with every log he picked up. It hurt plenty, and it was hard pretending that I didn't feel it. Jim was having the same trouble with the Russell kid, although the target there seemed to be Jim's knee.

We were only about a quarter of the way through the cord when the door swung open and the kids all piled out and headed for home. My hip was throbbing, and I was sure I must be black and blue six ways to Sunday. We just stood there taking the jeers from the kids hurrying off before we brushed off our hands to join them. Before we could take a step in that direction, Miss Drysdale was in the doorway.

"Don't even think about it," she said. "I'll be here working for some time. You boys keep on till every log is in its place. And fix that far corner. It's crooked." She stepped back inside, pulling the door closed behind her.

We had hardly spoken to each other except to utter a cuss word now and again, and the cussing got more choice as we watched the other kids leave. The next whack from Roger's log nearly knocked me off my feet, and I was explaining to him exactly what I intended to do with him when Jim put his log right square in front of where the door opened out.

"You can't put it there, you jerk," Roger said with disgust. "She won't be able to open the door."

Jim said nothing, but he carefully placed his next two logs on either side of the first. As he stood, he gave me a wink.

"The door opens out, you idiot!" Michael said, and he picked up one of Jim's logs to move it.

"Don't even think about it," I said, using Miss Drysdale's words if not her voice.

Michael put the log back down as I carefully placed my log right beside Jim's.

Roger was a bit brighter than Michael. He only glanced at me as he placed his next logs on top of mine without hitting me with them first. Even Michael caught on then, and we worked quickly. It seemed like no time at all before the pile of logs in front of the door went right up to the top of it.

I'm not sure just what Miss Drysdale was working on in that schoolroom, but it must have involved some heavy pounding. We could hear her at it as we headed home.

HORRIBLE! HUGE!

I still think the woodpiling incident was worth all the trouble we got into at school. We had to move that pile eight times around the schoolyard the next day before Miss Drysdale said it was in the right place. By that time we'd made friends with most of the boys, and things were settling down.

I'm just sorry Miss Drysdale had to go and tell our folks about it. Jim and I had to do dishes for the next three weeks, no matter how many guests we had, and muck out the stables every morning before school. We had no time and no energy to cause any more ruckus at home or at school.

It was Aunt Winnie who caused the next fuss. Very early one morning we heard her yelling and screaming. We were just behind Uncle Clint as he ran through the kitchen in his night-shirt. Aunt Winnie was leaning against the back door. The stovepipe had fallen, so she and everything around her were covered with soot. Some oatmeal was dripping down from her hair, and more ran down her apron front from the pot she held to her chest, making a line in the soot. She'd stopped screaming, but her eyes were big and she was breathing hard.

"What is it, Winnie? What's happened?" Uncle Clint asked as she fell into his arms.

"Huge!" she gasped, and hid her face in his chest.

"What's huge, Winnie?" Uncle Clint pulled her face up toward him.

"It came right after me. Oh, Clint! It was horrible!"

Mother and Dad had arrived in their nightclothes. Dad stepped behind Mother when he saw the source of the commotion. Never one to rouse quickly in the morning, he seemed to be having trouble focusing.

"Which fool said her food was horrible?" he asked, looking at each of us accusingly.

"No one, dear," Mother said. "That's what *Winnie* said."

"Winnie said her food was horrible?" Dad asked. He lowered his voice to a whisper. "Was it that lamb thing again?"

"Hush, dear," Mother said.

Aunt Winnie sobbed louder.

Uncle Clint reached around his wife for the door handle.

"Don't leave me, Clint!" she said, grabbing him tightly. "It chased me all the way from the garbage ditch."

"Good thing," Dad said. He whispered loudly to us all. "She threw that lamb thing in the garbage."

"It charged out of the woods like a house afire."

"Fire?" Dad shouted. "Boys, grab the pails! I'll rouse the guests." He started for the stairs.

"No, dear," Mother said, pulling him back by the tail of his nightshirt. "Nothing's on fire, and there are no lodgers today."

"It chased me," Aunt Winnie said. "All the way from the garbage ditch."

"The garbage ditch is on fire?" Dad asked. "How did that happen?" He thought a moment. "Was she burning that lamb thing?"

"Where's Rex?" Uncle Clint asked.

"Asleep at the foot of my bed," Jim said.

"Hmmph! Some watchdog," Uncle Clint said. He tried again to go out the door, but Aunt Winnie wasn't about to let go of him. Uncle Clint motioned over her shoulder to the rest of us.

"Better see what's out there," he said.

"Yes," my father said as we headed out the door. "And grab your shovels, boys. We'll bury the fire."

"There's no fire," Mother repeated. "Winnie saw something."

"Ah," Dad said, nodding as if he understood. He grabbed an ax.

Jim and I lined up behind my father, and Dad cautiously opened the door. After a brief look in all directions, we took slow steps forward. As nothing horrible and huge appeared, we grew braver and split up to search the area.

Mother took that time to explain to my father what was

77

going on. Whatever it was that Aunt Winnie saw or thought she saw was nowhere in sight. The ground was dry, and there were no footprints.

We came back inside to report. Father put the stovepipe back up. Uncle Clint tried to get Aunt Winnie to tell us more about the huge and horrible thing. She said it was awful and that it had a beard, and then she burst into tears again.

"Grace," Dad said over his shoulder as he went down the hall toward their bedroom, "see to Winnie."

"I don't care," Aunt Winnie said that night before we all went to bed. "It chased me, and I'm never stepping outside that door alone again."

She stuck to it. She stayed in the lodge except when Uncle Clint or Mother was by her side. Even then she made somebody inspect all the bushes and trees around the dooryard before she'd step out the door.

HIDE-AND-SEEK

The night of Jim's eleventh birthday, he got out of doing the dishes. When the rest of us finished the chore, he said, "Let's play hide-and-seek."

Mother smiled. "You and Frank have time a little while before bed. Go ahead."

"I mean everybody," Jim said. "Let's all play."

"No, dear," Mother said. "Hide-and-seek is a children's game."

"Why?" Jim asked.

Rooshy was on his way out the door when he stopped and said, "Yeah, why?"

"Why is it a children's game?" Mother asked. "Well, I don't know. Adults just don't do that sort of thing."

Uncle Clint stood up and grinned as he looked around. "Lots of good places to hide," he observed. "It's Jim's birthday. Why not? I'm game."

"Not it!" Rooshy said as he walked back into the room.

"Not it!" Jim, Uncle Clint, and I called out almost all at once.

79

Mother looked at Aunt Winnie. "Not it," she said softly.

Aunt Winnie's eyes were big. She looked quickly around. "Not it," she said with a giggle.

We all turned to gaze at my father, who was lost in the newspaper.

"What?" he said, bringing the newspaper down to eye level. "You think I'm going to play a foolish kids' game? Pshaw! When pigs fly, maybe."

"Bet you a new harness for Prince that you can't find everybody," Uncle Clint said.

"If I find everybody, you'll buy a new harness?"

Uncle Clint nodded. "We have to set a time limit."

"I knew there'd be a catch," Dad said. He brought his newspaper back up, then down again. "How long do I have?"

"Let's say an hour," Uncle Clint answered.

"It's dark out. I'll never find you in these woods. Too many places to hide."

"Make it a rule. Can't go outside," Uncle Clint said.

"You have to hide inside this lodge. I have an hour to find you, and you're betting a new harness that I can't do it?" Dad asked as he folded his newspaper and stood up.

"You've got it," Uncle Clint said. "It's nine o'clock. Start counting to a hundred."

We took off in all directions as my father closed his eyes and began counting.

"No peeking," Rooshy warned as he headed down the hall.

Jim was small enough to squeeze into the biggest bureau drawer in an empty guest room, and I pushed it in almost all the way before I headed for the back of the deepest closet in another room.

I was the second one Dad found. Rooshy declared that it was only because he needed to spit that he allowed Dad to find him first behind the sink in the laundry room. Mother and Aunt Winnie were in the same room under a bed, so they were a double find.

It was fun seeing all those grownups acting like kids. My father wouldn't have found Jim when he did if Jim hadn't giggled as Dad entered that room. That left only Uncle Clint. We all just stood and watched my father getting more and more frustrated as he retraced his steps and searched every room several times.

"Under something. Got to be. Dang foolishness," he muttered as he went by us for the third time.

"Do you know where he is?" Jim asked me. I shook my head. Mother did, too. Aunt Winnie just smiled.

"Give up, Fred," Mother said when he began his fourth round of search. "It's quarter to ten. You're not going to find him."

"Witnesses!" Dad said. He sounded almost like Jim when he's beaten at a game. "Rules! Broken them. In the woods somewhere. Bet's off. No fair."

"You're giving up, then?" Aunt Winnie asked, interrupting his muttering.

Dad went back upstairs. The clock finished striking ten when he came back down.

"He's broken the rules and ruined the game. He's nowhere in this lodge," Dad announced.

Aunt Winnie pointed toward the ceiling, and we looked up to see Uncle Clint looking over the center beam high over our heads. Heaven knows how he got up there, but getting down meant swinging from beam to beam to the wall over the balcony, and Uncle Clint cackled all the way.

SHOUTS AND SILENCE

As the weeks passed, guests came and went. Their number varied. When the big table was extended as far as it could be and every chair was full, there were so many conversations going at once that you could barely hear yourself think.

One night we had only four guests, but things got kind of noisy anyway. The men were all from Boston and had a lot to say about Boston politics. They'd all worked on Curley's campaign for mayor. He'd been defeated in 1917 but was apparently going to run again in a couple of years.

Why the matter of who was mayor in Boston made any difference to my father, I couldn't figure out. Maybe the fact that Curley was a Democrat had something to do with it. Anyway, things were already pretty tense around the table as they all got into it, and then Mother spoke up.

"By the next mayoral election," she said, "women will have the vote. What will you do to get their vote?"

"Send them a bunch of flowers," a guest named Freeman said. "Foolishness, anyway. Women voting. Let them stay behind the stove where they belong. Women have no business sense. That's a proven fact."

My father opened his mouth to speak but another of the men, Mr. Norris, spoke first. "They'll never get thirty-six states to ratify the amendment. That's the only reason it finally passed the Senate. They know it will never become law."

"It didn't take Massachusetts long to ratify, did it?" Mother remarked.

"Even if women do get the right to vote," Mr. Freeman said, shaking his head, "they'll just vote the way their husbands tell them to. It won't make any difference."

"If only," Dad muttered.

"If women get the vote," Mr. Norris said, "say goodbye to liquor. They're all temperance bound. The whole thing's backed by the Women's Christian Temperance Union. Vote women and you vote dry."

Mother pushed her chair back and stood. "Women who've had their lives ruined by drunken husbands are understandably concerned," she said. She started clearing dishes, motioning Jim and me to help. She pushed through the swinging door so hard it swung back and forth three or four times.

She was sputtering to Winnie as we began to stack and scrape dishes.

"Fools!" she said. "I'm so sick of ignorant men who are so

sure they know what women will think and do. And for politicians like them"—she motioned toward the door—"to say
things like that . . ." She slammed a tray onto the counter.

"Why do you care so much, Grace?" Aunt Winnie asked.
"Why do you even want the vote? You have such a nice home
and family." She looked around and wavered a minute. "Well,
you have a nice family, and waiting back in Montgomery you
have a home." She sniffed. "We both do."

"What does having a home have to do with it?" Mother
asked. "You can say that about Clint and Fred and probably
those fools in the living room too. They have homes and wives
and children. Why do they want to vote?"

"Well, it's different for men. They have a head for politics."

Mother turned an angry face toward Aunt Winnie.

"How can you say that, Winnie?"

Aunt Winnie busied herself with the dishwater. "Well,
President Cleveland said it was unnatural for women to vote."

"Unnatural?" Mother was furious. "President Cleveland was
a man! What did he know?"

"Well, of course, he was a man. We certainly wouldn't want
a woman . . ." Aunt Winnie's voice trailed off as she looked at
Mother's face. You had to give Aunt Winnie credit for arguing
with Mother. Not many did. She put another stick of wood in
the stove. "There are lots of women against it, too, Grace. I
saw a picture of their New York headquarters in the paper.
They think it's unnatural, too, the article said."

"Unnatural to want a voice in what goes on in this country? Unnatural to want to make sure that President Wilson's League of Nations is approved? That his Fourteen Points are adhered to? The future is at stake, Winnie! It's for a better world for Jim and for Frank and every other person, male or female. Unnatural, my foot!"

Mother grabbed a tray of desserts and used her foot to shove open the door as she headed back into the dining room. Jim and I stayed in the kitchen with Aunt Winnie. With Mother in a mood like that, it seemed the safest place to be.

Whatever Mother said got the shouting going again. It got so loud we could hear it way down in our bedroom later that night, and I think Mother and Dad continued the argument by themselves in their bedroom later.

Most times around the lodge were much more peaceful. Guests went riding, hiking, and swimming. Sometimes in the evenings they played whist or bridge or just read and talked. Sometimes people sang. Aunt Winnie played the organ while Jim or I pumped. Other times everybody'd play charades or twenty questions.

Jim and I had our own games, of course. At recess at school we played war a lot. Back at Yokum we built the fort and took turns being the Germans or the Yanks attacking it.

Then there was an awful time when things were too quiet at Yokum.

When Jim and I heard that a whole group of veterans was

coming, we thought we'd hear lots of good war stories we could use for our own war games.

When the wagons bearing the soldiers pulled into the yard, Rex ran out to greet the arrival as always, wagging his tail and barking. But then he seemed to sense something was different. He sat right down and watched them being unloaded. Some were in wheelchairs. Others walked with canes or crutches. Three nurses came with them.

Once inside the lodge, the soldiers just kind of stared into space. The nurses didn't talk much either, except to speak softly to the men as they pushed them around in wheelchairs. A few of the men walked around the place a bit, but for the most part I don't think those men knew or cared where they were.

"What's wrong with them, Uncle Clint?" I asked one morning.

For once there was no grin on Uncle Clint's face. "They've been gassed, Frank."

"Gassed?" I asked.

He nodded. "At the Battle of Ypres," Uncle Clint said. "Mustard gas was released over the trenches. It's poison. Chokes 'em. Tears up their lungs."

"Will they get better?" I asked.

"Some will," he said.

After that Jim and I sort of lost interest in playing war. We abandoned the fort.

WOMEN

Since no guests were due until the following Wednesday, my father and Uncle Clint decided to go to Montgomery one Saturday to check on things. At my father's insistence, they'd be taking the horse and buggy. That meant they'd have to stay in Montgomery overnight. Jim and I wanted to go with them to see our friends and Samson and Patch. Aunt Winnie said seeing it all would only make it harder to leave Montgomery again, and that's why she wasn't going with them. Jim and I thought about that and decided not to go either.

"Perhaps I'd better stay here," Uncle Clint said, "and see to the womenfolk."

A look from Mother ended that discussion.

"Besides," she said, "I've got some friends coming over this afternoon for tea."

"Friends?" Dad asked. "Folks from Montgomery?"

"No," she said. "People from up this way."

"How've you had time to make friends with all this work?"

"Oh, you know—on errands and at church."

Dad put down the box he was carrying and came over to Mother.

"Grace," he asked, "is it a women's suffrage meeting?"

Mother looked him straight in the eye. "Yes, Fred," she said. "It is. You don't mean to stop it, do you?"

"No," he said. "You do as you've a mind to. But, Grace?"

"What?"

"Just don't expect too much. This is Becket, not Westfield, remember."

"I will. Thank you, Fred."

My father nodded. "You boys be good now." He gave her a kiss on the cheek, picked up the box, and put it in the buggy. Uncle Clint got in; Dad clicked to Prince and off they went.

Mother told Rose and Martha to set up small tables in the main room with places for four at each place.

"How many tables?" Rose asked.

"Ten," Mother said.

"Ten?" Jim exclaimed. "That'll take fifty percent of the room." He'd been working on percentages at school and never missed a chance to show off. His smile of accomplishment quickly disappeared as he thought a minute. "Forty people are coming? Who's doing the dishes?"

"Forty people!" Aunt Winnie exclaimed. "Gracious! Did you send out invitations?"

"Yes," Mother said. She opened a drawer and took out a pink

paper. Under a copy of the painting *Whistler's Mother* that had the woman wrapped in chains, it said:

WOMEN! ONLY ONE MORE STATE TO GO BREAK FROM YOUR CHAINS! COME TO AN ORGANIZATIONAL TEA	YOKUM LODGE TUESDAY, JUNE 1 2:00 P.M. BRING A FRIEND.

Aunt Winnie read it aloud. "Who did you give this to, Grace?"

"Twenty people."

"And you think they'll all come."

"Well, wouldn't you?"

"Even if they all come, Grace, that's only twenty people."

"Look down at the bottom of the notice. It says 'bring a friend.' And that makes it . . ." She looked at Jim.

"One hundred percent more," Jim said quickly.

"Whatever shall we feed them?" Aunt Winnie asked.

"We'll just do up a few pound cakes," Mother said. "We'll serve slices of cake with blueberry sauce. That will do just fine."

❧

At two o'clock, the main room was all set up with ten card tables bearing shining dishes for four. A vase of wildflowers stood in the center of each table. A pink napkin folded like a fan was at each place. Aunt Winnie taught Jim and me how to do that. The first napkins were fun to fold, but after that it got tedious. Six pound cakes were sliced and waiting on covered platters in the kitchen beside the ten small pitchers holding the blueberry preserves. Ten teapots were ready by the stove.

Mother had set up a podium and an easel by the fireplace. On the wall behind them was her map with the stars on the states that had voted to ratify the amendment. Tennessee was colored red. Since Delaware had defeated the amendment, all hopes were on Tennessee. On the easel Mother had a large poster with a picture of the flag bearing the words of the amendment: "The right of the citizens of the United States to vote shall not be denied or abridged by the United States or by any state on account of sex."

Aunt Winnie and Mother were seated on the bench in the dooryard waiting for the first guests to arrive. Jim and I had been told we must disappear when the women came, but we could watch from the balcony. Our male presence, Mother said, might otherwise hamper the discussion. Rose and Martha were waiting at the back of the main room to begin serving when so ordered.

It was nearly two-thirty when a shiny yellow Buick pulled into the yard. Mother and Aunt Winnie stood to greet the two women who stepped out. Jim and I whipped around the corner out of sight.

"It's Mrs. Upton and Mrs. Meadon," Rose said. She and Martha were peering out the window as we came in through the back door. "Big wigs. Uptons own the thread mill, and Meadons own two of the paper mills. Pretty fancy company, boys."

Mrs. Upton was dressed in blue, with a wide-brimmed hat that had more flowers on it than were on the tables, and Mrs. Meadon had three red birds on hers. Jim and I took off for the balcony.

"I'm glad they're finally getting here," Jim said. "Mother was looking worried."

"Yeah," I agreed. "Guess folks just arrive late to things around here."

"Do you think there'll be enough leftover cake for us?"

"Sure hope so," I said as Martha showed the two ladies to a table up near the podium.

Rose brought in a teapot, and Mother poured their tea.

After a while Jim said, "Gosh! Do you think that's all that's coming?" His eyes were wide. "Mother will really be upset, won't she, Frank?"

I was about to speak when Aunt Winnie came in with another lady.

"Jimminey!" Jim whispered. "It's Miss Dried-up."

Mother went over to welcome Miss Drysdale and brought her over to the table with the other two ladies.

The clock on the mantel sounded louder than usual as it

struck three. Mother and Aunt Winnie had a whispered conversation in the doorway. Then Mother motioned to Rose and Martha. They brought in one pitcher of blueberry sauce and one tray of cake. As they served, Mother sat down with the ladies. She whispered something to Rose, who looked surprised and then whispered to Martha. Martha went out to the kitchen and came back with Aunt Winnie and another teapot. The three of them sat at the next table. Mother passed the cake platter over to Aunt Winnie, picked up her fork, and began eating and sipping tea. The ladies followed suit.

I had to give Mother credit. She chatted with Miss Drysdale and the other two ladies as if they were the only invited guests and not just the three loners who'd shown up.

Jim and I got bored and got out the checkerboard. Jim had jumped three of my men when Mother pushed back her chair and stood up.

"I'd like to thank you all for coming," she said. "I must say I'm disappointed with the size of the group, but perhaps it's just as well to start with a small group of committed women. I have some leaflets here about ways to support our sisters in Tennessee . . ."

Mrs. Meadon and Mrs. Upton folded their napkins and stood up.

"Thank you so much," Mrs. Upton said. "We have to be going."

Mother protested. "But we've just begun to . . . I thought . . ."

"Yes," Mrs. Meadon interrupted. "This was lovely. So nice to meet you."

She touched Mother's arm. "You go ahead with your little meeting," she said. "Perhaps these others will be interested."

"You understand," Mrs. Upton said, holding up the flyer, "we have no need for this. We leave the politics to our husbands."

"But it's so important," Mother said. "We must organize rallies, raise money, and write letters to support the battle in Tennessee."

"Perhaps you'd get more people to come to your meetings if you did flower arranging. That's very popular," Mrs. Meadon offered.

"Or a cooking class," Mrs. Upton added. "That was delicious cake. You must give me the recipe. So nice to see you again, Miss Drysdale." And with that, they left.

Mother looked about to cry when Miss Drysdale said, "You'd better start the meeting."

"Meeting?" Mother erupted. "Meeting? There is no meeting. Why did they bother to come?"

"Oh, probably to see who else would show up," Miss Drysdale said, "but you have four women here who have come . . ." She stood and moved over to Aunt Winnie's table. "Have come for a women's rights meeting. Let's see what you have here."

Aunt Winnie and the maids looked surprised, but they smiled nervously as Miss Drysdale sat beside them.

"This is so disappointing," Mother said. She pulled up a chair beside Miss Drysdale. Jim and I went back to the checker game.

The women were going through a stack of posters when Mother said, "Miss Drysdale, thank you for doing this."

"Let's make that Veronica," Miss Drysdale said.

Jim's head shot up. "Veronica!" he whispered. "Is that her name? Veronica Dried-up?"

"Must be," I said, looking out through the railing. I'd never thought about her first name. I don't suppose I thought she had one.

Mother smiled. "Veronica it is then. And I'm Grace. This is Winnie, Rose, and Martha."

"Oh, I know Rose and Martha. I had them both in school," Miss Drysdale said.

Both girls smiled. "Hello, Miss Drysdale."

Mother asked, "Why didn't the women come?"

"Lots of reasons, I suppose," Miss Drysdale replied. "Ignorance, disinterest—some are scared. Most of the women probably didn't know about this meeting and wouldn't have thought it had anything to do with them if they did hear about it. Girls, did your mother know about this?"

Rose and Martha looked at each other. "Well, we told her there was a party," Martha said, "but I don't think she knew it was a meeting."

Rose added, "She's awfully busy."

Martha nodded. "She's usually just finishing up the laundry about now."

I noticed that both Martha and Rose spoke up quite clearly when they answered Miss Drysdale.

"Where did you hand out the fliers?" Miss Drysdale asked Mother.

"At church and on the street in Lee," Mother said. "I thought we'd start small." She looked around at all the empty tables. "Little did I know how small."

"Which church?"

"Becket Congregational."

"Lots more churches than that around here," Miss Drysdale said. "We'll have to get to them all. And we'll have to try the mills their husbands run"—she nodded in the direction in which the two women had just left—"over in Lee and Woronoco. Women in the mills know about protest. Some of them are union."

"Will the bosses let me in?" Mother asked.

"Not on your life." Miss Drysdale shook her head. "We'll have to be at the fence before seven to get the women on the way in and at five when they come out. They can't stop us if we stand outside the gates."

Mother was nodding and writing on a pad. She stopped and looked up at Miss Drysdale.

"We," Mother said. "You said 'we.'"

Miss Drysdale pointed and counted. "Rose, Martha, Winnie,

you, and I," she said. "That makes five and . . ." She looked up at us. "I'm sure two strong and able boys like Franklin and James will be more than willing to help. Won't you, boys?"

"Yes, Miss Drysdale," Jim and I said in unison, speaking clearly down through the railing.

"All right. We'll start with the mills in Lee Monday morning," Mother said.

"What about the farm wives?" Rose asked. "You're still not going to reach people like Ma."

"You're right, Rose. We must find a way to get to the farmers' wives," Mother said. "You and Martha can get fliers to your neighbors, can't you?"

The two maids nodded.

"That'll help, but there are many, many more," Miss Drysdale said. "You'll get some of them at church. Except for the Grange and church, farm women don't get out much. Handing out leaflets to groups of women may create some interest, but convincing women around here that the suffrage movement has meaning for them is going to take more than leaflets. You're just not going to get many of those women to come to a meeting some strange lady is holding."

"They're kinda wary of strangers," Martha agreed.

"So what do we do?" Mother asked.

"I think," Miss Drysdale said, "we'll have to go door to door and spend most of our time talking and, even more importantly, listening to what these women have to say."

Jim and I grinned at each other. Listening was not one of the things Mother did best.

Miss Drysdale went on. "You see, Grace, for most women up here, whether or not women get the vote just doesn't matter."

"Doesn't matter!" Mother sputtered.

Miss Drysdale smiled. "Talk and listen?"

"Yes, yes," Mother said, folding her hands in her lap. "I'm sorry. I'm listening."

"So, we'll get them talking and we'll listen, and then we'll tell them, not about a rally, not about a march, not even about a meeting. We'll help them see what it can mean to their lives when women have the vote."

"What can it mean?" Aunt Winnie asked.

"It means being legally considered a person," Miss Drysdale said. "A whole person—not just Adam's rib. We'll tell them how to convince their husbands that women must have the vote."

"And how will we suggest they do that?" Mother asked.

Miss Drysdale laughed. "I read somewhere that Lucy Stone said, 'When he says good morning, tell him you want to vote; when he asks what you are going to have for dinner, tell him you want to vote; and whatever he asks from the time you get up in the morning until you lie down at night, tell him you want to vote.' We'll tell those housewives that."

Even Aunt Winnie smiled then.

"Door to door it is then," Mother said. She stood and began

to gather up the papers. "We will do that after the mills, the rest of the churches, and the Grange hall."

"The problem is," Miss Drysdale said, "I'm only available before and after school and on weekends. I'm afraid most of the work falls on you."

"That's all right," Mother said. "Winnie and I can start the door to door and you, Martha, and Rose can join us on weekends."

After Miss Drysdale left, we came downstairs. Mother sent Martha and Rose home early.

We were doing the dishes when Aunt Winnie put a plate on the counter and said, "Grace, I can't."

"Can't what?"

"I can't go door to door. I can't."

"Of course you can, Winnie. We'll all help more with the kitchen work, and you'll have time."

"It isn't that, Grace. I'll write letters, stuff envelopes, but I can't . . . It's . . . All those strangers. I just can't." She burst into tears and left the room.

Mother looked sad for a moment and then took the phone book. She sat at the table and began making lists of names.

Every morning Mother would come bustling in the back door just as we were sitting down to breakfast, having spent the early hours handing out leaflets at the mills. Sometimes she'd make Jim or me come with her, but I think she got sick of hearing us complaining and let us sleep.

She went to several organizational meetings in Pittsfield. Those meetings plus all the farm calls kept her busy, and we saw very little of her except at mealtimes.

One night, after we were in bed, I heard Mother and Dad arguing in their room.

"Grace," he said. "You've got to cut back on the voting stuff. You're a wreck. You hardly get any sleep."

"Cut back?" she said. "How can I possibly cut back when there's so much yet to be done? I just got a pack of new leaflets to hand out. We haven't even touched the homes in Lennox. Each visit takes so long, if the women will talk to us at all. If their husbands are around, most of them give us short shrift and a slammed door. Even if their husbands aren't there, some of them don't want to talk to us. But, oh Fred, some of them do talk, and some of them have such terrible lives. It would break your heart, Fred. The women in the mills would, too."

We could hear Mother opening and slamming drawers.

"There's so much to be done, Fred. Even after this amendment passes, the work's only started. Those women in the mill —they work right alongside the men and get paid half of what the men do. Women schoolteachers over in Pittsfield get a third less salary than men teachers. Because, they say, because men have families to support!"

"I know, Grace," Dad said. "It isn't fair."

"Of course it's not fair. What about those widowed women with children? Don't they have families to support? What about single women with ailing parents?"

"I know, Grace," Dad said. "I know. And I'm not telling you to stop, but, Grace, you're wearing yourself to a frazzle and letting things here get out of hand."

"Out of hand? How can you say that? I do the books every morning before I leave for the mills. I've been here every single night for supper except for that time I had the flat coming back from Pittsfield. It's so hard, Fred. Most of them think I'm just a pest, some fruitcake at the door interrupting their housework."

"Grace, I know you're trying, but you're losing track of things. Winnie ran short of yeast yesterday and—"

"Yeast! I'm engaged in changing the lives of women everywhere, and you talk of yeast?"

"Shhh," Dad said. "You'll wake the boys. Let's go out on the porch."

They did and I heard no more.

EXCURSIONS

Rooshy finally got around to taking Jim and me to the Indian rock ledge. Jim was sure we'd see Indians there and wanted to bring a shotgun, but Mother put the kibosh on that. It was a place on the side of the hill where boulders had been rolled up to form a wall around a place in front of a cliff. On the other side of the boulder wall there was a space not really deep enough to call a cave. Overhead the rock had been chipped away to make a flat kind of ceiling. We didn't believe Indians had been there until Rooshy poked his foot around in the gravel at our feet and uncovered some broken arrowheads. We spent a couple of hours there and found quite a few arrowheads. Some weren't even broken. I put mine on cotton in a glass frame and hung it on the wall over my bed.

One night in July, Rooshy finally took us down to the haunted house. We'd been by it in daylight, of course, and it was spooky even then. The windows and doors on the ground floor were all boarded up. Some kids had thrown rocks and broken some of the upstairs windows. It was creepy, all right. We crouched in the bushes and watched lightning bugs flicker. The mosquitoes made their presence known in their own sweet way.

"Does the ghost walk every night?" Jim asked.

"Nah," Rooshy said. "Only when the moon is full."

We looked up at the crescent of a moon.

"Shucks," Jim said. "Guess we won't get to see any ghost tonight."

"Guess not," Rooshy said. "Hope we haven't disturbed him none though."

"Why's that?" I asked. I hoped my voice didn't tremble as much as Jim's had.

"Well," Rooshy said as we stood up and headed for home, "if we'd disturbed him, he might follow us home."

"Why?" Jim whispered. "Why would he follow us home?"

"Hard to tell," Rooshy said. "They say whistling will scare away a ghost."

"Whistling?" Jim squeaked. "But I can't whistle." He looked at me for help. I just shrugged.

"Do your best," Rooshy said. "It's all a man can do."

Jim and I took every occasion we could to look behind us on the long walk back to the lodge, and boy did we whistle all the way, though I doubt any ghost could have heard Jim's whisper whistle.

I was almost asleep that night when I heard a slight rattle from over near the window.

I sat up in bed and peered through the dark room. A faint light came in the window from the light over the doorway below.

"Just imagining things, I guess," I said to myself, and settled back to sleep. It came again a little louder: *rattle, rattle*.

I thought Jim was asleep and was trying to decide whether or not to wake him up when he said, "What is it?"

"Beats me," I said. "Probably just the wind."

"Wind's not blowing," Jim said, sitting up and pointing toward the still tree branches outside.

We sat on the edge of Jim's bunk. In the silence it came again: *rattle, rattle*.

"It's the pitcher," I said. "It's rattling against the bowl. Must be off balance." On the table by the window a water pitcher sat in the big bowl just like in all the other bedrooms in the lodge. It was mostly for decoration. We never used it.

I got up and moved the pitcher slightly and went back to Jim on the bed. *Rattle, rattle, rattle.*

"Jimminey!" Jim said. "It's Old Man Barnes. He's followed us home." He began his whispering whistle.

"To rattle our pitcher?" I asked.

"To let us know he's here, I guess," Jim said. "Whfft! Whfffft!"

I'd like to say that I never believed that for a minute. I'd like

to say that I didn't run into Mother and Father's bedroom and make them come into ours. I'd like to say that I knew it was just Rooshy trying to scare us even before Dad showed us the thread going from the handle of the pitcher under the window to the outside, where Rooshy was crouched against the house. I'd like to say that, but I'd be lying.

REVENGE

It rankled Jim more than it did me, getting spooked by Rooshy like that. Jim spent a lot of time thinking up ways to get even.

One late afternoon we were taking a quick dip in the lake before supper, and I gave up chasing a very clever frog to see Jim standing there waist-deep in the water and muttering to himself just like Dad. "Short-sheet his bed," he said. "Doesn't use sheets." Jim splashed his hand away from himself as if throwing out each idea. "Set fire to his clothes." Splash. "Hide his tobacco." Splash. "Glue his jaws together so he can't spit." Splash. "Pull his last tooth." Splash.

"Hatching a plan?" I asked.

"Gotta get him back," Jim said without looking up. "Put salt in his coffee." Splash. "Hide his liquor." Splash.

"Don't you want to scare him?" I asked. "Seems like you should be trying to think of a way to scare him the way he scared us."

Jim looked up from his contemplation of the water. "Yeah," he said. He nodded several times. "Right." Splash. "Scare him." Splash. "Make him scream." Splash. He laughed wickedly. "Make him cry for his mama."

I shook my head, grabbed my towel, and headed back inside for supper. Mother had to call Jim three times before he came in, but he was still muttering.

This went on for several days. Then the muttering stopped, and Jim got very quiet. He had a faraway look in his eyes.

That night Jim sat on the edge of his bunk, his eyes shining and a smile on his lips as he went through a pile of stuff he'd taken from the back door entryway: hats, long coats, and a couple of scarves. He also had a jar of Mother's cold cream, a box of talcum powder, and a whisk broom.

"Here," he said, handing me a hat and coat. "Put these on before you put on the cold cream and powder." He was slathering cold cream on his own face and then powdering it with talc, making it shiny white.

"You think the sight of us in these clothes with powder on our faces is going to scare Rooshy?" I shook my head. "I don't think he's that easy to scare."

"Anybody'd be scared if he looked out his window late at night and saw this!" Jim said. He lit the lantern and shut off the room light, then held the lantern under his chin. He did look kind of spooky.

"What do we do to wake him up?" I asked. "Whistle?"

I was kidding, but Jim took it seriously.

Jim doused the lantern. "No," he said. "I can't whistle good enough. We'll scare him with this." He held up the whisk broom.

I laughed. "I know Rooshy doesn't like to clean, but I doubt if the sight of a broom will scare him."

"Not the sight." Jim grinned. "The sound. Listen." He went over to the window and brushed the glass with the broom. It did make a weird whishing sound.

"Oh well," I said. "It's a nice night. Might as well give it a try."

A few minutes later Jim and I crouched outside Rooshy's window. Slowly we raised our heads just enough to peek inside. The full moon was shining, and we could just make out the form of Rooshy's body on the bed. He was lying on his side with his face to the wall.

"He can't see us, even if he opens his eyes," I whispered.

"This'll make him turn over," Jim whispered back.

He lit the lantern and handed it to me. "Hold it up under your face," he whispered. He put his own face right next to mine at the window and began to brush the window with the broom. *Whisk. Whisk.* We watched the bed carefully. No movement.

Jim whisked the broom against the window.

"He sure is a sound sleeper," Jim whispered. I nodded and motioned toward the broom.

"Again," I said.

A noise behind us made us turn around. In the moonlight, we could see it. Coming slowly out of the woods near the lake was an old man carrying a lantern in one hand and a scythe in the other. A long rope dangled almost to the ground. He began to moan.

I swore I was the first to start running, but when I slammed the back door of the lodge, Jim was under the stovepipe when it fell.

For a while neither of us said a word as we got out the stuff to clean out the mess.

Finally Jim spoke. "I'll never doubt Rooshy's stories again," he said.

I nodded and handed him the dustpan.

Jim started sweeping and then stopped. "Rooshy!" he said. "What if the ghost got Rooshy? We should go back and help him." But he made no move toward the door.

I just stared at him.

"Aw," Jim said as he began sweeping again. "Rooshy can probably take care of himself. Right?"

"Right," I said. "Let's go to bed. Dad can put the pipe back up in the morning."

BERRIES AND BEES

In August when the blueberries began to ripen, Aunt Winnie sent Jim and me out each morning to get enough for pies. She refused to pick them herself because of the huge and horrible thing. One morning when the season was in full swing, Uncle Clint insisted that we go over to Washington Mountain, where the picking was better.

"Lots of high-bush berries over there," he said.

Mother agreed to take a day off from politicking. Aunt Winnie and the maids stayed at the lodge getting ready for a large group of guests that were coming in the next day, but the rest of us, including Rex, climbed into the wagon for the blueberry picking.

Rooshy kept us entertained on the way with his tales about rattlesnakes. He said they were all over Washington Mountain. Jim was wide-eyed and, I must admit, I was a bit uneasy myself. We'd had a few rattlers in Montgomery, usually around our stone walls, but they'd rattle if they heard you coming and were no problem if you watched where you put your hands.

The problem was, Rooshy said, rattlesnakes in deep grass around the blueberry bushes would be hard to spot. Then Rooshy mentioned bears. Turns out that bears are as fond of blueberries as humans are, and, he said, Washington Mountain had almost as many bears as it did rattlesnakes.

Mother suggested that we turn back, but Dad said neither the rattlers nor the bears would be a problem because we made so much noise any critter would hear us coming and vamoose. He also said that Rex would be a match for any bear. There was some discussion about that.

Rooshy declared that was probably true, but just to make sure, we should all sing while we picked.

We sang every verse of every song we could think of that day. Rooshy knew some good songs, but Mother stopped several of them partway through in spite of our protests.

I don't know how the rattlers and bears felt about our concert, but my father declared that anyone who even hummed "Found a Peanut" again was due for a trip to the woodshed.

We picked a lot, and we ate a lot. Most of all we sang a lot. Everybody but Rex, who spent most of the day chasing rabbits, was hoarse and had purple fingers and purple teeth at the end of the day.

Then Mother screamed. We all rushed over and, at first, we laughed because she was doing this funny kind of dance, hopping around and slapping at herself. It took a minute to see the bees that were all over and around her. We started over toward her but she screamed, "No, go back!" She began to run.

My father took off his coat and ran after her. He threw his coat over her, patted her all over to crush any bees, and then picked her up and ran with her to the wagon. We jumped on as Dad picked up the reins and clicked to Prince, and we headed for home at a fast trot.

"Are you all right, Grace?" Uncle Clint asked. He reached his hand toward her, but didn't quite touch her.

Mother's voice was muffled under the coat. "I . . . I think so," she said.

For a while there was no sound except the soft thud of Prince's hooves on the dirt road and then: "Do you have the berries?" Mother asked.

"Never mind the damned berries," Dad said. He clicked his tongue and Prince began to gallop.

Mother's face peered out from the coat. "Get the berries," she said. "I'm not going through this for nothing."

Dad turned around at the next pull-off, and we went back to pick up the pails we dropped, scooping up as many of the spilled berries as we could. We'd lost some, but there were still many buckets of blueberries in the back of the wagon when we pulled back into the dooryard of the lodge.

Mother, still covered with the coat, hurried inside with my father close behind her.

"Put some baking soda on those stings!" Uncle Clint called after her.

We started unloading buckets. "Winnie!" Uncle Clint called out as we piled out. "Come see what we've got!"

"Probably seeing to your mother," he said when Aunt Winnie didn't come. We all went down to see how Mother was.

She sat on the edge of the bed. Her face was all swollen. One eye was nearly shut. My father handed her a wet cloth.

"Shall I fetch Doc Wilson?" Uncle Clint asked.

"No," Mother said. "I'll be all right. Fred, get the tweezers. We should get these stingers out."

Dad went off to find the tweezers. Mother winced as she placed the cloth over her eye.

She waved us away. "Get those berries in the icebox before they mold," she said, "and let me nurse my wounds in private."

Things were cooking on the stove, several lids rattling, but there was no sign of Aunt Winnie when we went through the kitchen.

Jim and I brought the berry pails in and placed them on shelves in the icebox. Uncle Clint was getting worried.

"Where could she be?" he asked. "Winnie?" he yelled. "Boys, go see if she's with the maids."

But she wasn't. Rose and Martha said they hadn't seen her since dinner.

A quick search of the lodge turned up nothing, and we all

wandered around the outside, calling and whistling until Uncle Clint said, "Hush a minute."

When we got quiet, we could hear a faint voice. "Clint, oh Clint." It was coming from the outhouse.

Uncle Clint ran over and opened the door, and Aunt Winnie stumbled out.

"Winnie," he said. "What happened?"

"It wouldn't let me out," she said. She was holding on to Uncle Clint with both hands.

"What wouldn't?"

"That thing!" she said. She stopped and looked around at all of us. "It was here!" she declared. "Every time I tried to come out, it ran at me."

"The horrible thing?" Uncle Clint asked, biting his lip.

Aunt Winnie looked straight at him. "It ran at me," she repeated, daring him to laugh.

He didn't. "What did it look like, Winnie?"

"It was huge! And horrible! And it had a beard," she said.

"Could we get a bit more information?" Uncle Clint asked. "Was it some kind of cat?"

"A cat?" Aunt Winnie was outraged. "You think I'd be this scared of a cat?"

"Well, I didn't mean a house cat," Uncle Clint explained. "I was thinking more of a wild cat or—"

"Are wild cats taller than you are?"

"Taller than me? The thing that chased you was taller than me?"

Aunt Winnie nodded. "I told you it was huge," she said. "Didn't you hear me? It was huge. It was horrible. It had a beard, and it chased me."

"Did it have a rope around its neck?" Jim asked.

Aunt Winnie just stared at him.

"Seems to be a day for being chased," Dad said as he came out the back door. "Winnie, if you've recovered your senses, perhaps you could see to Grace."

"Grace? What's happened to Grace? Where is she? Has she been hurt?" Aunt Winnie asked, her own fright forgotten in her concern for Mother.

"Stung," Dad said. "Very badly stung."

"My land! Poor Grace! Why didn't you tell me?" Aunt Winnie turned on her husband.

"Well, Winnie, it was hard to get a word in edgewise what with the screaming and all."

She shook her head and hurried inside.

Uncle Clint started in after her and then turned back to my father.

"Is Grace all right?" he asked.

"Think so," Dad said. "We got most of the stingers out, I think. Still, she's pretty swollen and sore. Enough excitement for one day. Grace and the bees and Winnie with her mysterious beast."

"Do you think she really saw something?" I asked. "Bigger than Uncle Clint?"

"Of course she saw something," Jim said. "Why would she spend all that time in the stinky outhouse if she didn't?"

"Remember, this is the woman who's afraid of a chicken," my father said. "She probably saw a deer."

Uncle Clint shook his head. "She's seen deer at our place. I won't say she cottons to them, but she wouldn't be this scared." He thought a minute. "A beard. She said it had a beard. What kind of animal has a beard?"

"Old Man Barnes?" Jim asked.

"Whatever it is," Dad said, "let's hope she doesn't see it again. We could lose a good cook."

MOTHERHOOD

We didn't see much of Mother the next few days. Dad said she didn't want anybody to see her with her face all swollen. She took her meals in her room. As if the stings weren't bad enough, she broke out all over with hives. She finally let my father call Doc Wilson from down in the village. He came right over. He said she'd be all right but she'd better stay away from bees, or the next time it could be worse.

"Worse!" Dad said. "She's swollen up like a pig on a spit, for goodness' sakes! I don't see how it could be much worse."

"Just be careful," Doc Wilson warned. "People can die from bee stings. Sometimes if a person has been badly stung like Grace has, they develop an allergy to stings. Another bee sting could kill her."

"He's just telling tales, isn't he?" Jim asked after the doctor had left. "Like Rooshy does, right?"

None of us believed the doctor. We all knew bee stings hurt, and we could just imagine what it felt like to be stung with a lot of them, but fatal? Hardly. Still, Mother resolved to stay clear of bees.

She was back in public again by the time the next guests came, although she still wore sunglasses, even in the house.

On August 18, Tennessee ratified the Nineteenth Amendment, and we all celebrated. Mother was triumphant, and the rest of us were relieved. Dad made the mistake of saying that now that women had the right to vote, Mother's hard work was over.

"Over?" Mother asked. "Over? Why, the work has just begun. We need to work for equal pay for women, equal protection under the law. There's tons to do. We've barely started. We've got a big meeting coming up in Pittsfield next week to plan the next step."

Dad left the room muttering.

Whatever it was Aunt Winnie had seen, we had a lot of fun with it. We took to calling it Horrible Huge, and Jim and I warned people to beware of the bearded giant anytime anyone went out the door alone. Every new guest had to be told the story about Aunt Winnie and the beast, although we were careful not to tell it when she was around.

Rooshy was the only one who took it seriously. He said that he'd seen many horrible and huge things in those woods.

Aunt Winnie didn't seem to be comforted by that, and my father said that Rooshy might see fewer strange things if he cut down on the whiskey. Rooshy pretended not to hear him.

Rex caused a ruckus one morning while we were all eating breakfast with the guests. Mother had gone down to Lee to get some groceries.

"What's he barking at?" Dad asked. When we all shrugged, he hollered, "Rex! Hush!"

Rex kept on barking, and finally Dad put down his fork and went to the back door.

"Hey!" he called. "Come see this."

Aunt Winnie was turning pancakes, but Uncle Clint, Jim, and I went out. Rex had cornered something that looked like a deer, only it was a grayish-brown color and had much longer spindly legs.

Dad called to Rex, but it took some time before the dog left the critter and came to my father.

"Think that's Winnie's creature?" Uncle Clint said.

"Probably," Dad said. "That's a woman for you. A young moose! Nothing to be scared of."

"It's kinda cute," Jim said. "But it can't be what Aunt Winnie saw. She said it was taller than you, Uncle Clint, and that thing isn't much taller than Frank."

"No beard," I said.

"Women exaggerate, son," Dad said. "But they're going

to vote." He shook his head and began to mutter as we all stared at the thing that stared at Rex. "Women . . . Expect to vote . . . Need a clear head."

Rooshy came up from his cottage.

"Watch out for mama," he said.

"Mama?" I asked. "Whose mama?"

"That one's," Rooshy said, pointing to the young moose.

"It's got a mama?" Jim asked.

"Most everything does," Rooshy said.

"Nowhere in sight," I said, looking around.

Rooshy looked doubtful. "If there's a baby around, then mama's not far off."

A light seemed to dawn on Dad. "This mama," he said. "That would be big, wouldn't it?"

"Oh yes," Rooshy said.

"But a beard?"

There was no time for further discussion. All of a sudden there was a crashing noise in the bushes, and then a blur of motion as a very big moose gave the young one a shove back into the bushes. The little fella didn't argue, but as soon as it was out of sight, that thing turned her attention to us.

It was huge. It was horrible. It had a chunk of skin and hair that hung down like a beard on its chest, and it ran right at us. Rex yelped and took off into the woods in the opposite direction. The rest of us stumbled all over ourselves and each other getting in the door. My father had me by one arm and Jim by

the other. He shoved us ahead of him into the house and slammed the door behind him.

That jarred the stovepipe loose, adding to the commotion as that moose hit the back door full force. The door was solid oak but it fell in like cardboard. We hightailed it through the kitchen. Uncle Clint grabbed Aunt Winnie on the way. He pushed her on in front of him as the moose came right through the little room and was halfway into the kitchen before it seemed to think the better of it. It shook its head and backed away, stepped over the fallen door, and was gone.

"If that's mama," Dad said, "I'd sure hate to see papa."

"I thought moose had antlers," I said. "I've seen pictures of them, and they don't look like that."

"Mamas do," Rooshy said.

"Do they only act like that when their babies are in danger?" Jim asked.

"They act worse when they're protecting the young, but a female moose is meaner than a mountain lion."

We looked at Aunt Winnie for comments, but she just nodded her head and began to clean up the soot while Uncle Clint put the door back on its hinges and Dad replaced the stovepipe.

LOSS

One night Jim and I lay in our bunks listening to the crickets that'd begun their late-summer call.

"Are you asleep, Frank?" Jim asked.

"Nope."

"Remember how we fussed about coming to Yokum?"

"Yep."

"It's been fun, though, hasn't it? Mostly, I mean."

"Yep."

"Think we could talk them into staying here all winter?"

"Supposed to close down after Thanksgiving."

"I know, Frank, but it's more fun here. We could have Christmas here. We can string lights on the deer heads and put a gigantic tree in the main room. We could . . ."

Jim probably kept talking, but I must have fallen asleep.

❧

It was a Saturday afternoon in late September, and we'd had several killing frosts, but the weather had turned warm again.

The guests were with Rooshy, fishing on the lake. Uncle Clint and Aunt Winnie had gone into Pittsfield for the day, and the rest of us were having sandwiches on the porch. Mother brought out some iced tea.

"Did you go to Lee this morning?" I asked.

"Yes," she said, pouring us each a glass. "I wanted to be at the shoe factory when they let out at noon."

"It's after three," Dad said.

"I know," she said. "One of the women asked me to come talk to her sister at home."

"Her sister doesn't work?"

"She did, until she came down with lung disease from breathing the air in the combing room. She said some days the air in there was so thick with flying flecks of wool that it was like being in a snowstorm." She filled her own glass and stood looking out over the pond. "There are so many women yet to reach. And they all have such busy lives that it's hard to get them to care about politics. But they have to see that it does matter. It really does." She sat down in one of the wicker chairs, with the glass in her right hand, and then quickly pulled up her left arm. "Ouch," she said.

"What?" asked Dad.

"I don't know," Mother said, and rubbed her upper arm. "Something stung me, I guess."

She pulled up her sleeve to reveal an angry red spot just below her shoulder that was beginning to swell.

"Good thing it's only one this time," Jim said. "Remember when you got stung with all those bees?

"I certainly . . . do," Mother said. She looked puzzled.

"Are you all right, Grace?" Dad asked. He got up and walked over to her.

"Yes, of course," she said, but she didn't look all right. Her face was red, and she was breathing funny.

"I . . . just . . . can't seem . . . to catch . . . my breath."

Dad picked her up and headed for the back door.

"Get Prince," Jim yelled.

"Too slow!" Dad yelled over his shoulder as he ran toward the Ford. "You drive, Frank!"

I was sputtering as we ran to the Model T. "I can't drive up here."

But Dad was already in the back seat with Mother. Jim grabbed the crank as I got behind the wheel. I had driven, of course, with Mother a few times, but never without her telling me what to do and never on these curvy mountain roads.

The car started on the first try. Jim jumped in, and we sped off. I headed for Doctor Wilson's house in Becket Center. I don't remember the drive except for Jim's occasional "Watch it!" when we were heading too close to something. I know I took some of those curves too fast, but nobody said a word. Even at that speed it took forever, but I finally pulled into Doctor Wilson's driveway. Dad was out of the car with Mother

in his arms. Someone opened the door, and he dashed inside.

"She'll be all right, won't she?" Jim asked.

"Of course," I said. "Doc Wilson will know what to do."

But he didn't. Dad said that Mother had stopped breathing before we got there, and nothing anyone could do would revive her. She was gone. Our mother was dead.

❧

Somehow we got through the next few days. People came and went. Most brought food that sat untouched on the big table in the kitchen. We cried a lot. Sometimes just one or two of us would break down in sobs. Other times everybody cried at once. Sometimes we'd fall into exhausted sleep in our beds or wherever we happened to be. Then we'd wake up, and the nightmare would go on.

Dad decided she should be buried in Montgomery since she had so few friends up in Becket. It didn't matter. Jim and I went around like robots, sitting when they told us to, moving wherever they told us to go.

It was Uncle Clint who finally sat down with us to talk about it. He explained that Mother had died of anaphylactic shock, that that one lone bee sting had triggered the allergy that was set up when she had been so badly stung before. I guess that made some kind of sense, but it didn't seem to matter to either Jim or me. All that we knew or cared about was that she was gone and nothing would ever be the same. And, of course, it wasn't.

On Saturday, September 18, we drove down with Dad in the surrey with Prince. Aunt Winnie sat in the back with one arm around Jim and the other around me. Uncle Clint was up front with Dad. After a silent ride, we pulled up to the church in Montgomery.

The church was crowded, but my eyes were so full of tears, I didn't see anyone clearly. I didn't try. There were flowers everywhere. You could hardly see the casket for all the flowers on and around it. We walked straight down to the front pew. The minister began to talk as soon as we were seated. I don't know what he said. Then he stopped talking, and Miss Drysdale came and stood in the front of the casket. She was dressed all in white, and she wore the purple and yellow suffragist banner. Rose and Martha came up on either side of a woman who must have been their mother. Then other women came to stand beside them. They were all wearing white. Some wore the whole white outfits while others had just a white blouse or apron over their housedresses. They all wore homemade banners in various shades of purple across their chests.

Jim whispered, "Jimminey!"

There was a lot of rustling behind us as, one by one, women from Montgomery got up and joined the mountain women around my mother's casket.

Nobody said a word. They didn't need to.

AFTER

Uncle Clint and Aunt Winnie went back up to Becket until the season closed. Dad, Jim and I went back to the house in Montgomery. Jim and I went back to school. Dad learned to cook some other things besides tripe, and Jim and I, with Aunt Winnie's help, managed to put food on the table. Things got back to as close to normal as Dad could make them. It wasn't easy, but we managed.

Eventually I went off to college and a few years later, Jim did. Then Jim took a job in Boston, where his wife ran for city council. I set up medical practice in Maine. Dad married again and seemed happy. Jim and I worried about what to call his new wife. We couldn't call her Mother, and it didn't seem right to call her Veronica. So we called her Miss Drysdale, same as before. She did all the driving. When the Equal Rights Amendment campaign began, there was a lot of driving to do.

None of us, of course, ever forgot those few months at Yokum Pond. So many of those memories would make us shout with laughter as we recalled them over the years. And the memory of all those women standing in the little church in Montgomery still sends tears coursing down my cheeks. She was quite a woman. It was quite a time. We came to Yokum and that changed everything.